FIRESIDE TALES
OF THE
TRAVELLER CHILDREN

FIRESIDE TALES
OF THE
TRAVELLER CHILDREN

Duncan Williamson
Edited by Linda Williamson

BIRLINN

This edition first published in 2009 by
Birlinn Limited
West Newington House
10 Newington Road
Edinburgh
EH9 1QS

2

www.birlinn.co.uk

First published in 1983 by Canongate Publishing Ltd

ISBN 978 1 84158 814 8

British Library Cataloguing-in-Publication Data
A catalogue record for this book is available from the British Library

Typeset by Hewer Text UK Ltd, Edinburgh
Printed and bound in the UK by CPI

Contents

Preface

Born 11 April 1928 on the shores of Loch Fyne across from the Manse of Sandhole, Argyll, Duncan Williamson was the seventh of sixteen children. Their parents, Jock and Betsy Williamson, were Travellers, well-known throughout Argyll for at least fifty years after their marriage in 1914. The Williamson family travelled no great distances because Jock's first priority was to have his children schooled – to be literate, something he was not. He returned to the same place every winter for thirty-seven years to build a barrikit (a large tent, see Introduction, p. 1) in the oak wood in Furnace on the Duke of Argyll's estate, though during the summer holidays the family wandered the Highlands between Lochgilphead and Inveraray (except from 1939–1945 during the war), lending a hand in farm work and hawking their tin and natural willow wares.

At the age of fifteen Duncan decided to leave home with an older brother with whom he walked to Perthshire. That was the beginning of his travelling, which continued until 1980, when he moved into a farm cottage in Fife so that I (his second wife and an American postgraduate student) could record and transcribe some of his vast oral repertoire of songs, stories and folklore.* We have two children and

---

* Highlights of Duncan's biography and a fine appreciation of his life as a Scots tradition bearer are featured in an article by B. McDermitt and A. Bruford in *Tocher 33*, published by the School of Scottish Studies, University of Edinburgh, Spring 1980.

Duncan has seven by his first marriage to Fife Traveller Jeannie Townsley (1932–1971).

For forty years Duncan Williamson has been consciously carrying a tradition and keeping alive an ancient and vital oral literature, a quality for which he is honoured by his own people:

> I was always special among the Travelling folk for my stories and songs, since I was fifteen. I travelled Forfarshire, Aberdeenshire, Inverness-shire, Argyll-shire, Perthshire, Ayrshire and Fife – meeting hundreds of Travelling families before and after I was married in 1949. I've been at their ceilidhs and at their fires, I've listened to their stories, sung their songs, learned their tales. I was singing around the Travellers' campfires from the age of fifteen, telling and collecting their stories. Everybody wanted me to sing and tell stories to them.

Since I have been married to Duncan, his reputation as a traditional narrator has become international. His storytelling activities as well as his singing reach far beyond the listening ears of kith and kin. From appearing as a guest artist-storyteller to scholars attending international conferences on narrative research, to sharing his wealth of traditional knowledge with children in primary schools throughout Scotland, Duncan Williamson's art has helped bring recognition to a part of Scotland's heritage, only ten years ago thought to be lost indefinitely.

Virtually everything on the following pages is in Duncan's own words, transcribed from taped recordings made during the past seven years which have been deposited in the School of Scottish Studies Sound Archives, and edited by myself with the help of Dr Alan Bruford of the School of

Scottish Studies and Stephanie Wolfe Murray of Canongate, so far as to be comprehensible to a wide English audience.

The first four stories were narrated on different occasions to members of Duncan's family and were told in fairly straightforward English. 'The Hedgehurst' is a story with international parallels; themes and motifs can be found in the Aarne-Thompson folktale catalogue, AT 441. In the Highland story 'Mary and the Seal', Duncan imitated Highlanders' talk. Some of the repetitions, speech phrases and stammering were incorporated in the text. Turns of phrase and vocabulary more peculiar to the Travellers give 'White Pet' its fresh appeal; it is a well-known traditional story, AT 130. The goat in Duncan's version of 'The Goat that Told Lies' (AT 212) speaks English for the most part. Occasionally it slips into Scots, following the narrator's dialect, when it furthers its deceitful ploy of endearing itself to the old man and woman. Many Traveller cant words and phrases were retained in 'The Traveller Woman who Looked Back', a story sharing motifs with other international tales. In the two Jack tales, Scots phrases and Traveller idioms were left intact e.g., saying the opposite of what one means; these are crucial to the characterization of Jack – the Travellers' hero. Burker stories are a cornerstone of Traveller culture; and 'The Boy and the Boots' (AT 1281a), a direct quotation from Duncan's father's narration, follows his exact speech. Completing the storybook is 'The Pot that went to the Laird's Castle' (AT 591), in a language far from normal English. The narrative was a 'true story' told by Duncan to an illiterate Traveller friend; it portrays a very typical Traveller family and lifestyle, current among the Travelling People of Scotland until the middle of the century.

We should like to thank the following for their support

and assistance in preparing this collection of Traveller children's stories: the Scottish Arts Council, Mr Robert Williamson (Worcester), Mr D.M. Young (Cupar), Mr David Clement (Edinburgh), Mrs Mary MacDonald (Edinburgh), and Dr Alan Bruford (Edinburgh).

Linda Williamson
Kincraigie, Strathmiglo, 1983

Preface to the Birlinn Edition

After the rousing American edition of *Fireside Tales of the Traveller Children* by Harmony Books, New York (1985), it is a pleasure returning Duncan's first book to Edinburgh for this publication by Birlinn. The text of *Fireside Tales*, a masterful record of Scotland's storytelling art, has been expanded to nineteen tales, recorded from Duncan Williamson in the height of his work with children from the 1970s–90s. 'The Coal, the Straw and the Bean', 'The Two Trees', 'True and Untrue', 'The Tramp and the Bull', 'The Boy, the Toad and the Snake' and 'Death and the Woodcutter' have not been previously published. 'Archie's Besom' was one of twelve tales recorded and published by Central Regional Council in 1987, a literacy project for the Traveller children, who illustrated each story with drawings of pure magic.

Introduction

I. The Traveller Children's Way of Life, 1914–1955

Life was always hard for the Traveller children, the youngest members of an outcast minority group with a history that predates written records, but the hardest time was at the beginning of World War I when their fathers were called to the army and their mothers were left alone to take care of them. They needed their fathers because Travellers were very very poor in those days, without the luxurious caravans, cars, lorries and televisions many have today.

In winter they stayed in one place in a barrikit, a three-part structure made from strong saplings bowed and tied, covered with canvas and other suitable materials, anchored to the ground with big ropes and rocks. The barrikit was dome-shaped, twelve feet high with a hole at the top for the fire-smoke, and fifteen feet across, with room for seating up to twenty people. Kitchen tables were on one side, trunks and boxes on the other side for clothes, keepsakes, the man's pipes, tinmaking tools and so on. There was plenty of headroom for standing, hanging up rabbit skins and wet clothes. The floor was earthen with an open fire in the middle – 'if the fire wasnae shared you werenae welcome'. On either side of the dome were smaller bow tents (also used while travelling in the summer) made from young rowan, birch or hazel saplings bound together at a height of about five feet. These were the sleeping quarters separated by entrance covers from the main barrikit. One was for the children, one for the parents and possibly another for a family relative. A drain was dug around the whole structure to channel away rain and melting snow. Before the family started travelling again, the barrikit was burned and a new one made the following autumn.

Some families took houses. But in the month of March, or April, when they moved off, every child would have to help carry something – a certain amount of clothes, canvas, sticks and string to tie the sticks for the bow tent, a hatchet for splitting logs, a saw for cutting firewood, the snotem, the tea kettle, cooking utensils and basins for washing at the riverside.

A Traveller father would never force a child to carry a bundle on his back all day but in the morning he would advise each to do their part for the journey ahead. Travelling was really hard – I mean, you were tired and you wanted to sit down to rest but your father kept walking on. He had a big bundle on his back and your mother probably had a baby on her back, another in her oxter. All the children were strung out behind like chickens after a hen. Father would say, 'Come on, children, carry on.' We would say, 'Daddy, Daddy, have we got far to go yet?' His answer, 'Just a wee bit, just a wee bit . . .' It was always a wee bit! I remember walking over a large hill with my father and mother. I was really hungry and I was behind. I had this bundle on my back and in it was the tea kettle. I sat down and ate the leaves out of the kettle with hunger.

No food was carried; the mother would have got their food as they went. She sold the father's handmade wares, baskets or tin items, at farmhouses or in villages. If she couldn't get money she traded them for food: she would prefer this, because shops were very far between.

When the father came to a camping place he'd lay down his bundle and say, 'Children, we're staying here for the night.' The children took all they were carrying and left it down beside his bundle. He would say, 'Children, you know what you've got to do!' Right, some would go for sticks, some for water. While he put the bow tent up – one long enough to accommodate all the family asleep – and while the children brought firewood, the mother kindled the fire.

If she didn't have any bread she'd say, 'Children, you'll have to wait a wee while, until I make a scone.' They'd say, 'Mummy, we're terribly hungry, we came a long way today and we can't wait for a scone!' 'Well,' she said, 'I'll make a pancake for you.' So she would make a big flapjack (large thick pancake) and a pot of tea.

'Now, children,' the father would say, 'you know you cannae lie on the cauld ground. Before you get started playing you'll have to go and gather all the nice grass you can get.' So each would gather a wee handful of dry grass and put it in the tent. Then the mother would lay a canvas cover on the ground, pack all the grass on top of it and lay another cover over that for the beds.

After the fire had been kindled, the tent was up and they'd had something to eat, it was a new world for the children: gone was their tiredness and they'd play away – climb trees, hunt for rabbits or guddle for trout (if you were a laddie about seven or eight years old), or gather flowers (if you were a lassie) and play till the evening came in. But once the father put a finger in his mouth and gave a whistle, you were better to come in – if you weren't back after the second whistle you got a beating.

By that time mother would have supper made. They all sat round the fire; there were no tables or chairs, spoons, knives or forks. The mother carried ten or twelve tin plates the father had made and one ladle for putting meat on the plates. No matter what the children got to eat, they ate it with their fingers.

Then the mother would make the bed at the very back of the tent for the youngest ones, the two- to three-year-olds who were usually sleepy. The father would go for his bundle of sticks – oh, you should have seen what he could carry on his back! He picked all the big thick sticks and packed them on the fire, right close to the tent outside the door. (The bow tents had no inside fires.) The children all sat round the fire and as the night got darker they crept in closer! They got kind of frightened if they were in a strange place, but the father would always keep his big tools for making tin wares lying beside him in case he should need them for defense. Then they would say, 'Daddy, tell us a story.' He'd say, 'Well, come on there, weans, gather round, I'll tell ye a story.' He would always sit down beside the fire with the bundle of sticks beside him; he'd keep putting them on the fire, the sparks would go away up in the air . . . he'd start telling a story. He might have told them a ghost story to make them quiet and stay close. I remember when my father was telling us a real chilling ghost story, we'd turn our backs to the fire, because we believed the ghost couldn't come through the fire to our backs, and if he came to our faces we could see him!

So he would tell stories until one by one sleep would take them all – each wean got a story after the day's journey. The father would put them to their beds, two at the top and two at the bottom of the tent, feet touching each other, until everyone was comfortable. The father and mother would sit and have another cup of tea before bedtime. And maybe the father would light his pipe. Then he'd say, 'Well, thank God for the day,' and he would go to his bed.

During the summer months it was likely that four or five Travelling families would meet in the one camping place (until the mid-1950s when large numbers of the Travellers' traditional camping sites – regularly used by certain families for centuries – were closed or destroyed by those in authority). If families were related to one another, their tents would be built in a circle around one fire; otherwise the tents were spaced wider apart with separate fires. At night-time after supper, the men would get together around the fire. They would start talking and telling cracks, short stories, to each other. One would say, 'I ken a story for the weans', and they would come in close to the fire – suppose there had been a dozen you could have heard a pin drop. One might lift his wee baby into his lap, another would lift his, maybe one man would have two, one in each arm. In fifteen or twenty minutes these two would be asleep and he would say, 'Wait, boys, don't go away, I'm only taking them to their mother.' They would have fallen asleep at the fire listening to the story, and he would say to their mother, 'Put them to bed.' He would go back to the fire, the cracks and stories would start again. And they told stories till every wean fell asleep.

Although life was hard for the Traveller children, they did not really suffer – no pain or torture. The only suffering was when they were on the road and there came a day of rain – with nowhere else to go but below a tree where they might have to stand for hours till the rain went off. It might have been a place where the father could not put a tent up.

The most terrifying aspect of life for a Traveller child would have been the encounters with schoolboard officials which sometimes resulted in a child being taken from their parents, brothers and sisters, and put away to homeschools.* The law required 120 days in school annually for each child aged between five and fourteen. But some districts were stricter than others. Dumbarton, Greenock, Paisley, Glasgow (and for thirty miles around), Ayrshire and Stirling were areas where Traveller children were taken to homeschools. It didn't matter if the children were dressed like bene hantle,† the police made the family stand in the road while the Cruelty Inspector said, 'Look, you and you never attended school (if there was no proof to the contrary) – right, get into the car – off to the home!' Many of the children of Travelling families ended up there before and after World War I.

But some districts didn't bother. In Perthshire, Angus, Fife, Argyll and Aberdeen the authorities maintained that the Traveller children weren't suffering as long as they were along with their mummies and daddies; they had their tent, had their bed, had something to eat and their mummies and daddies to love them. Travellers often went up glens around Aberfeldy, Killin, Pitlochry and Perth and no-one cared if the children weren't in school, for they were helping their fathers and mothers. That's all the education they needed – to learn how to survive. But the children who were interested in schooling got books and taught themselves if they wanted to.

* Officially named industrial or day industrial schools, homeschools were not orphanages or boarding schools; but were certified institutions (thirty in Scotland at the time of World War I) operating until 1937 after the Day Industrial School Act, 1893, where tinker children would have been committed if their parents were found to be neglecting their education, in accordance with Section 118 of The Children Act, 1908. See the *Report of the Departmental Committee on Tinkers in Scotland* (HMSO, Edinburgh, 1918).
† bene hantle – gentry

Traveller children were taught to work when they were five years old. The first job would have been thinning turnips on their hands and knees. From the age of three or four they experienced the labour by sitting on their mothers' backs and watching. Potato gathering was the most important contribution the young children made towards the family's maintenance – with all children chipping in, one week's pay might more than equal the total income of the previous half-year.

More valuable than learning how to read and write were the skills of the traditional trades that Traveller parents taught their children. Traveller women took their daughters with them everywhere, showing them every little quirk and corner of the hawking business. And hawking went on every day. If you didn't hawk, you didn't eat. The mother's main role was food supplier. If a young Traveller lassie did not know how to sell, to beg or go to the houses, her future was doubtful: young Traveller lads, potential husbands, might speak of her, 'Och, she's a bonnie lassie richt enough but what good is she? She's only fit for the country folk,* no good enough for a Traveller. What can she dae? She cannae beg or hawk or sell because her mother never trained her.'

Some Traveller women didn't train their daughters to hawk round the houses because they wanted them to find other lines of work, get off the road and be something. Once I overheard my mother say, 'Lassie, if ye live the life that I live ye'll never be any better; all you'll end up wi is a bing o weans† and dae the things that I've done.' Some lassies didn't want to do it because they felt deeply ashamed, and in these cases the mothers never forced them: it was not

* country folk – non-Travellers
† bing o weans – lots of children

uncommon for the village children to shout, 'Oh, look at the tinkies, look at the tinkies!' at a group of Travellers hawking around houses. But there were also young Travellers who weren't bothered by the rude remarks of the country folk. A lassie who was not taught to be a real Traveller woman very likely remained single until the age of seventeen or eighteen, which was considered old to be single. The lassie who was as good as her mother at hawking would have been snapped up by a Traveller laddie at a very early age, perhaps fourteen.

For a Traveller laddie there was no choice. It didn't matter what he could do, he was qualified to marry a Traveller woman. The fathers taught their sons every single thing – poaching, basketmaking, tinsmithing. The sons were the favourites. They were interested in whatever their fathers did: they knew if they didn't watch and do the things their fathers did, they couldn't do it for themselves when it came to their turn.

In the last few decades, the life of the Scots Traveller children has changed radically from how it had been for hundreds of years. In the fifties, after the Second World War, motors began to get popular with the Travellers; during the sixties caravans supplanted the tents because they were easily hitched up for moving. Then television, along with radio, came into vogue and Travellers had no more time for sitting around a campfire talking. Now the life of the Traveller is fading into the past.

II. The Importance of Storytelling to the Traveller Children

On cold winter nights when early darkness enclosed the old Travellers' camps, a father would turn round and take his children beside him. 'Listen, children, sit down and be quiet – I'll tell you a story.' My father knew in his own mind, at these times, that he was going to tell us something that was going to stand us through our entire life. Probably he had no tobacco for a smoke; probably we didn't have a bite of meat to eat, we had no supper. But we sat there listening to our father telling us a story and we were full, not full with food, but full of love of our father's voice. And even though he was hungry himself, he was teaching us to be able to understand what was in store for us in the future, telling us how to live in this world as natural human beings – not to be greedy, not to be foolish, daft or selfish – by stories.

Today as before, Traveller children are told different types of stories to correspond with their stage of growth. Between the ages of three and five a Traveller child hears stories about animals, such as the fox, the rabbit and the birds – stories in which the animals speak. From the very beginning a child is taught to be gentle and kind to animals, to love and respect creation. For everything a Traveller needs to know can be learned from nature: in their own environment in their own way, animals can take care of themselves.

The older child, from the time he is about six, hears many stories where the hero is called Jack – tales of fortune and tales of cleverness. In these stories Jack may be lazy and appear daft, but he is not too greedy or cowardly or bad. A Traveller child is taught to identify with Jack, to obey his parents, go his own way in the world and look for a living, not to expect too much, not to be a thief or murderer and not to be bad or the devil will get him. Devil stories, ghost stories and burker tales* are most suitable for children

---

* Burkers are defined in the introduction to 'The Boy and the Boots'.

beyond the age of ten. Younger ones would be too easily frightened by them.

Between the ages of twelve and fourteen, Traveller children are considered mature. Socially that means they are permitted to sit around the fire and listen to anything: then they are expected to sit like men and women, tell their own cracks (short, loosely formed stories on any subject) and longer stories. I'll always remember the impact a thirteen-year-old Traveller boy had made on his listeners, as he told his first story around the campfire. Everybody was telling tales and stories and this boy said, 'Daddy, Daddy, Daddy, I want to speak! I want to tell a wee story.' His father was a wee bit embarrassed. All the people around the fire said, 'Okay, son, come on, tell a story!' And you know, that thirteen-year-old boy, who is a man today, maybe a father of many children, started and told us a story – it wasn't a story he'd read in a book, it was a story he'd heard, a burker tale that had been passed down to him. And right at this fire in the heart of Aberdeenshire – there must have been twenty-four people – you would have heard a pin drop! The boy entertained us for nearly half an hour, till the end of the story, and I bet there wasn't one person round that fire who could have told it better than he did. Although we knew it! He told us and everybody was interested, not because we'd heard the story before, but just because we wanted to hear the way that he, a thirteen-year-old boy, could tell it. And it was great!

On summer nights when the large outside campfire used to be kindled and the children had gathered round, the Travellers would narrate animal stories to keep them entertained until eventually the little ones would fall asleep. As the young ones fell asleep the tales got bolder and stronger. Narrators would move from animal tales to stories about witches or, more often, the henwife,* and so on to burkers and ghosts. Exactly what to tell was left to the discretion of the tellers. Nothing was prearranged and a story might be about anything – a past experience, something that had happened in the teller's lifetime, or a traditional tale that had been transmitted through centuries.

While everyone around the fire had to take a turn telling something, a code of respect for the age and sex of the listeners determined the teller's choice of subject. Stories or cracks of an indelicate nature were reserved for later in the evening when young ones, particularly lassies, were not present. The code was open to interpretation; the tellers did not wish to offend anyone so they always introduced their stories, honouring the oldest and not forgetting the youngest listeners. A man might say, 'Well, I'm going to tell you a wee story . . . but it's not very nice – you've got a wee lassie.' The father who was listening with a daughter of five years old beside him might respond, 'Oh! Oh, don't worry about my wee lassie, she's okay – she understands.' He then wanted his child to hear the shameless talk, though what one man might have wanted his child to learn at the age of five another man might not have wanted his child to listen to at seven. It all depended on the maturity of the child.

Storytelling in Traveller society is not just meant for children. When I was twenty-four years of age, a grown man with three children, I sat with my brother and my cousins from ten o'clock one night until six o'clock in the

* Unlike the miserable witch, the henwife was a positive character: if hens and cockerels were picking round about a house, she would give the Travellers eggs and whatever she had. The generous henwife always helped the Travellers. They believed she had the powers to work the cures and the enchantments; and it seemed to be often the case, that Travellers' stories would more often include the henwife and not so often the witch.

morning listening to an old man telling us tales. We spent a full night listening to him and never noticed the time passing. He knew something about everything: he told us tales of the war, stories of his past, from his boyhood days, things he had heard sixty years before from his own family. He told how things were free and easy in his day, what it was to be happy and free. And we had a feeling of peace and freedom. We were just like Indians sitting on a mountain top – no cares in the world, we had nothing – just a voice from this old man whom we respected so much. He told us so many things, things of life that stood us in good stead through our entire days. I would give all the money in the world to go back right now to that night; the only difference would be, I would sit longer. Until the day that I die and leave this world I will remember him. And he knew in his own mind that he was telling us something that would be remembered years after he was gone. That was the way with all Travellers.

It's not just the story. It is something to last a person for his entire life, something that's been passed down from tradition: that's what stories mean to the Travelling people. They know their children are going out in the world, and some day they will be gone. The children need something to remember their forbears by, not monuments in graveyards or marble stones. The Travelling people know they are giving their children something far better: mothers and fathers know if their children follow the stories that they hear at the fireside, and live accordingly, then they cannot help but remember who taught them the stories. Travellers give you the tale so they will never be forgotten.

I've tried to teach my children the same tradition. I've told stories to them because I had the knowledge of tales and my children learned most of the good tales that I know. But whether they will pass the tradition on to their children is another thing . . . I don't know. Perhaps this first publication of the Scots Traveller children's stories will strengthen the case for hope in my children's children, and go a little further towards the education of yours.

The Hedgehurst

Once upon a time there was a woodcutter and his wife and they lived on the edge of the forest. The woodcutter's wife was often left on her own in this cottage by the forest and she was always wishing she had someone to keep her company because every day her husband was away cutting wood, timber, working well away from home. She used to go to the village every second day, when she needed some messages. She used to see all the kids playing in the street; she longed, longed very much for that baby of her own.

She said, 'I wish I had a little boy or a little girl.'

So every time she'd been away in the village her husband would know what he was in for when she came back. He said to himself, 'She'll probably be on to me tonight again when I return from work, about the same thing – wanting a baby of her own. But we've tried our best without any success.'

So he landed home and had his supper. He was sitting at the fire, by the kitchen window; it was a lovely evening . . . summertime.

His wife started again to tell him, 'John, I was in the village today . . .'

'I know you were, I can see that.'

'And you want to see the lovely children that run about there! I wish I had someone like that to keep me in company.'

'Well,' he said, 'get someone up from the village! Get a woman or someone.'

'I don't want a woman to keep me in company. I don't want anybody – I want a baby!'

'Well, we've tried our best to get a baby . . . we've never been blessed with one so far.'

'How I long for a baby, a boy or a girl – any kind of baby – suppose it was as beautiful as a snowflake, or as ugly,' she said, 'as that hedgehog feeding out there in the garden! I would love it just the same.'

But unknown to them, on her way home to the forest was a fairy, a wicked fairy. And she heard them. She stopped at the window-sill and they never saw her. She said to herself, 'Well, if she wants a baby, a baby she will get!' So after resting a while she flew on to her home in the forest. The woodcutter and his wife never knew anything about this.

Time passed by. And naturally, true to the fairy's word, the woodcutter's wife had a baby, a wee baby boy. And when it was born it was the ugliest little baby you ever saw! It had long, thick, dark hair on its back.

But the woodcutter's wife loved it. The woodcutter himself looked at it two or three times and he wondered and wondered and he wondered: it had a wee, long, sharp, narrow face, a wee straight nose, and its arms were short and its legs were short, and it had this long dark hair all the way down its back.

'Look!' he said to her.

She said, 'Isn't he beautiful?'

'Well, the way you've longed for a baby, anything would be beautiful to you! But to tell you the truth, I think he's really ugly.'

'Ooh – no, no,' said the wife, 'he's not ugly!' And she cuddled this wee baby to her breast.

'Well,' he said, 'so be it. If it makes you happy . . . it's your baby.'

But the wife really loved it.

As the days went on the wee boy grew and the more he grew the uglier he got. Till one year passed into two, and two into three and three passed into four and four passed into five. By the time he was five years old, his back from his shoulders down, and all his belly and chest in the front was just pure hedgehog – all over. His father despised him and hated the look of him. The hair on his head was just like a hedgehog's, and his face. But he had two of the loveliest blue eyes you ever saw! His mother adored him – she loved him! His wee legs were short and his hands were short. His mother would never let him out of her sight.

The father used to call him 'beast' every time he got caught. 'Get out of there, beast!' he would say to him. And this disappointed the mother, she hated it.

So one day when he was six years old, he came into the kitchen and his mother said, 'Come for your tea, son.'

And the father said, 'Give him a bowl of bread and milk – that's good enough for a hedgehog!' The boy just looked at him, said nothing.

Then he said, 'Father, I want you to go down to the blacksmith's and get me a saddle made.'

'What?' said his father.

'I want you to get me a small saddle to fit me!'

'To fit you?' said the father. 'What do you mean, to fit you?'

'Well,' he said, 'you'll go down to the blacksmith shop and get me a saddle and get me a bridle to fit the cockerel, my pet cockerel!'

Now this cockerel that the hedgehurst (or hedgehog-boy as you would call him) had, was about the largest cockerel you ever saw: it stood about three feet high. And wherever the boy went this cockerel went with him, he'd practically reared it since it was a wee chicken, this cockerel could do anything. And he used to get on its back. This is what he wanted the saddle for.

So as not to disappoint him, the next morning the father goes down to the blacksmith and gets a lovely wee leather saddle made and a bridle, and comes back and gives it to the boy. The boy bridles and saddles his cockerel, climbs on its back and drives it round the farm two or three times. When his mother saw this she was highly delighted, the father just shook his head in despair.

So he comes up, ties up his cockerel in front of the cottage and says to the father, 'Look, I want three hens, three geese and three sheep from you.' His father kept some geese in the forest.

'What for?' said the father.

'What would you do with these?' said the mother. 'You have all the animals here that you need.'

He said, 'I'm leaving tomorrow morning, and I'm going out into the forest to start my own kingdom.'

So the mother shook her head. 'Look, son, there's miles and miles of forest, hundreds of miles of forest here! You'll get lost and devoured by wild beasts.'

'I won't,' he said. 'I want to start my own kingdom. Father, are you giving me the sheep?'

'Help yourself to them,' said the father. He thought to himself, 'I'll get rid of him some way because I hate the look of him – he's half animal.'

So the next morning he picked out three of the nicest sheep he could get (two female and a male), three hens, two geese and a gander.

'There you are,' he said, 'take these with you wherever you may go!'

And his mother made up some food in a bag for him.

The hedgehurst saddled his cockerel, tied the bag of food over his back, drove his three sheep out in front of him and disappeared into the forest with his cockerel.

But he'd been gone for six months, then a year passed by, and the mother took to bed with a broken heart for her wee son and she died. The father gave up the cottage, married again and moved away to another country. Nothing was heard of the hedgehurst and his cockerel for twenty years.

Anyway, it happened that a king of a certain land had got lost in the forest: in these days there were miles and miles of forest, no roads or anything – he had lost his way. He himself landed in this clearing in the centre of the forest, and came to the loveliest house built of wood that you ever saw! All the trees were felled, all the place was lovely and green. And there were hundreds of the most beautiful sheep you ever saw, hundreds of hens and hundreds of geese! Right at the front of the house was this large cockerel, the largest cockerel he had ever seen! So the king stopped his horse, looked around him, he was amazed. He'd never seen anything like this before.

He said to himself, 'What kind of place can I be in?' And he shouted, 'Is there anyone there?' twice.

The third time a voice answered him, 'Yes, there's someone here, what can I do for you?'

'I am a king,' says the king, 'and I've lost my way.'

'And I am a king!' says this voice from the house. 'And I have not lost my way: you are now in my kingdom and you are no longer a king to me.'

'Come out and show yourself!' says the king.

So out stepped this young man – half hedgehog and half human being. And the king stood and looked: he'd never seen a creature like this in all his days.

He said, 'What type of being are you that could do all this? Have you anyone to help you?'

'No,' said the hedgehurst, 'I need help from no-one.'

'You mean to tell me,' says the king, 'that you built this place by yourself and you cut all these trees, built all these things and made this place like this?' It was the most beautiful place the king had ever seen.

'I have,' said the hedgehurst, 'I've done all this myself. But anyway, getting back to you: what is it you want of me, for I am king of this and this is my kingdom.'

'I want nothing from you,' says the king. 'But, I am amazed! Tell me, what are you?'

He said, 'I am a hedgehurst.'

The king said, 'I never heard of a hedgehurst.'

'Well, you're looking at one now: you see I'm half hedgehog and half man.'

The king shook his head; he'd never seen anything like this.

'Anyway,' said the hedgehurst, 'so that no-one can say I ever turned anyone away from my door, come in and have something to eat!'

So he took the king in, gave him plenty to eat, plenty of goat's milk to drink, and gave him plenty of mutton to eat and plenty of fowl. He had everything he needed, vegetables galore! And the king sat and he had the greatest feast he'd ever eaten in his life.

'But tell me,' said the hedgehurst, 'what put you here?'

'Well,' said the king, 'I was lost, on my way home.'

'Well,' said the hedgehurst, 'this is a forest for miles and miles and miles except the clearing, where you see I've cleared away this place. I've enough land here to do me and my animals.'

'It's a lovely place,' says the king, 'and you've got such a lovely house. But to get back to the point: I'll pay you well if you'll show me the road out of the forest, because I've been in here for three days and I'm just going around in circles.'

'Well,' says the hedgehurst, 'I could show you the road out of the forest, but it's many, many miles away from here. But I could direct you – if you make me one promise.'

'If it's within my power,' said the king.

'Well, you're a king. Anything's within your power. Do you promise me faithfully,' he said, 'that you will give me, to myself, the first thing that meets you when you land back to your own kingdom and your own castle – as I know what a castle you will have, you being a king?'

'True,' says the king, 'I have a large castle and a large kingdom.' 'It will be my dog,' says the king to himself, 'because he'll be the one to meet me, me being away so long.' So he shook hands with the hedgehurst and made a promise that he would give the hedgehurst the first thing he met when he came to the castle.

The hedgehurst led the king for three days through paths and swamps out of the forest. He shook hands with the king, bade him farewell and told him that he'd come for his prize in a year and a day.

So the hedgehurst went home and the king went on his way and rode home to his kingdom. The very first thing he met when he came to his own castle gates was his beautiful young daughter who was only seventeen. She threw her arms around her daddy's neck and kissed him for being so long away, and asked him where he'd been. Then it dawned on her daddy, his daughter was the first thing he'd met when he came back to the kingdom. So he goes up to the queen and the queen makes him welcome, takes him in, and he turns round and tells her his story about the hedgehurst that he came to in the forest.

'Well, you'll have to do something,' said the queen. 'You'll have to do something and put him to the sword.'

'I can't do that,' said the king, 'that's beyond my power. I could never do that. I'm a king, and my word is law to the people. If I fail one I must fail the lot. No, I must keep to my bargain, whatever may come or go,' he said, 'the hedgehurst must have my daughter.'

The queen was very sad at this.

But anyway, things fared well and the days passed and the months passed, and the king and queen practically forgot about the hedgehurst. Till a year passed, when one of the guards at the gate of the palace came running in and demanded to see the king.

'What is it!' says the king. 'What is wrong? Are we being invaded or something?'

'We are, Your Majesty, being invaded, but not by any army!'

'What is it, then?' says the king.

'By a flock of sheep, geese and hens coming from the forest! And sitting astride a large cockerel is the funniest person I've ever seen in my life!'

'It's the hedgehurst!' says the king. 'He's come for his reward.'

He sends for the queen and tells her. And the young daughter is trembling with fear of this creature called the hedgehurst, which she's heard so much about but has never seen.

'Anyway,' said the king, 'you'll go down there and you'll meet the hedgehurst and you'll find a place for all his animals and see that they're well taken care of. Get the soldiers and troops and people to look after his animals, and bring the hedgehurst to me!'

So it was, down went the guard who threw open the castle gates and told his troop of soldiers to find pasture and shelter for every animal. There must have been close to three thousand between them all; they were still coming in the next day with sheep, goats, hens and geese. And they were the loveliest animals that anyone had ever seen – the king was amazed at this.

So up comes the hedgehurst and tells the king, 'See that my cockerel is well taken care of, that he wants for nothing!'

'Right,' says the king, 'it shall be done! But first you must come in and meet my queen and daughter!'

'Very well,' says the hedgehurst.

Now the hedgehurst during his years in the forest had grown big, and he stood nearly a head bigger than the king, which meant that he was well over six feet. When he walked in with this long hairy back, hairy feet and hairy chest the princess and the queen fell back in fright.

'Don't be afraid!' said the hedgehurst. 'I'm not here to hurt anyone.'

So he sat down and talked to the king; and the princess hid her face in despair when her daddy said, 'The first thing I met was my daughter.'

'I know,' said the hedgehurst, 'I knew the moment you got home. And I've come for my reward.'

'So be it,' said the king. 'You shall have it!'

So he sent couriers all over the country telling everyone that tomorrow the young princess was getting married to the hedgehurst, half hedgehog and half man.

Everything fared well and the wedding went on, lasting for three long days, with drinking and merry-making. But the hedgehurst spent the first day in the garden roaming around and admiring the castle, never speaking to the princess till it came to bedtime; and up the stairs they went to their own bedroom. In the bedrooms in these olden days they kept large fires.

He said to the princess, 'You'd better get to your bed!'

So the princess went to her bed. She was lying in her bed trembling with fright of the hedgehurst. But she had nothing to be afraid of: when he saw that the princess was in bed he just walked over to the large fire, put more sticks on it (they were large pine logs), curled up into a ball and fell asleep by the fire.

The princess had been lying and had fallen asleep, and she must have slept till well on, till late at night, when she heard movements at the fire. And by the flickering light she saw the hedgehurst get up, pull the skin off his back, off his head, and go over to the corner – in the darkest corner – and dress himself in some of the king's clothes which he had brought up with him when he came up to his room. When she looked and saw him, she covered her head with the blankets and buried her face in the pillows because she thought he was coming to her ... but no – he never came near her.

The moon shone through the window and she looked, she saw him walking down the stairs and out into the night. He was away visiting his animals. And lying at the fireside was this hairy ball of skin. So, he must have been gone for about an hour when the princess heard him coming back into the room, back to the fire – took off his clothes, on with his skin, curled up into a ball and lay down by the fire again.

Now this went on for three nights in succession. He never bothered the princess in any way whatsoever. But the princess couldn't stand it any longer and she told her mother about all this.

The mother says, 'Don't tell your father ... We must go and see someone – we must go and see the henwife. She's the only one who'll know what to do.'

Away go the princess and the queen to the old henwife. When the henwife saw them coming she made them welcome because she had known the princess since she was a little baby.

'What is it, Your Majesty, that makes you pay me a visit,' she says, 'here at my home?'

'Well, I've come,' says the queen to the henwife, 'both the princess and I, with a problem.'

'What is your problem? I've just heard that you've been newly married, are you not spending your time with your husband?'

'It's my husband I want to talk about,' says the princess. And she tells the henwife what has been happening.

'I've heard about it,' says the henwife. 'I've heard about the hedgehurst, but I've never really seen one. I'll tell you what to do: you go back tonight, and keep a good fire on before you go to your bed. And if it happens, the same thing tonight that has happened the last three nights. . . . I'll give you a wee pitcher – now this is not any ordinary pitcher – you'll fill it with clear crystal water from the well, and you'll take it up to your room and hide it! You'll go to bed. And when he gets up during the night and goes out, you'll rise, and where he's cast his skin you'll put it in the fire – burn it! Then stand behind the door. When he comes in, you'll take this pitcher of cold clear water and you'll throw it over him – if it's a spell it'll be broken forever!'

'All right,' says the princess, 'I'll do that.'

So back goes the queen and back goes the princess to the palace, but they never tell a soul. The princess takes up the little pitcher of ice-cold water and hides it under her bed. She's quite happy the rest of the day and she talks to the hedgehurst and seems not to bother so much. Although the king's beginning to wonder if he'd made a mistake keeping his word to the hedgehurst, the queen's starting to treat the hedgehurst naturally, and the hedgehurst is feeling funny because they never treated him like this before.

So, it comes round again to bedtime. Up goes the hedgehurst to the stairs, up the stairs to his bedroom and up goes the princess.

'Right,' he says to the princess, 'get to bed!' And he builds up the fire.

The princess gets into bed but she's trembling with excitement – not with fright this time, but with excitement she's trembling. So she covers herself up and pretends that she's sound asleep. But just about twelve o'clock, the midnight hour, with the full moon (the light from the moon shining in through the window) and the fire burning bright, up gets the hedgehurst. He pulls off the skin from his back, off his whole body – off his feet, off his hands, off his face – right down, rolls it into a ball and leaves it down beside the fire. He dresses himself again in some of the king's clothes and slowly walks down the stairs. She never sees his face but she sees his back and she can see that lovely golden hair is hanging down his back. She says to herself, 'He must be a handsome young man.'

But anyway, she rises up, puts on her clothes, runs to the side of the fire, catches this hedgehurst's skin, puts it in the fire, flings sticks on it, pokes it with a poker till it's burned away to ashes, goes back and stands behind the door with the pitcher of cold water in her hand. She hasn't stood there for any longer than fifteen minutes when she hears the footsteps coming up the stairs. It comes to the head of the stairs, it stops – as if it knows that something is the matter and is afraid to come in through the door – just as it's coming in through the door she takes the pitcher of icy, clear water and throws it about him!

He gave a scream. And he turned around – she looked

at him in the light, she saw that he was the most handsome young man she'd ever seen in her life. And he walked over, put both his arms around her, kissed her and said, 'Darling, you've broken the spell that was cast on me many, many years ago!'

So the next morning he walked down and the queen and the king were surprised. So he told them the story. And the king and queen were very very happy. He told them:

'I am going back to my kingdom in the forest and I'm taking my princess back with me.'

'So be it!' said the king. 'But will you do me one favour before you go, and I'll give you some men and some troops to help you and plenty of people to look after both you and the princess: will you give me some of your fine animals before you go?'

So he gave the king some of his fine animals, and the prince went back to his kingdom.

And that's the last of the story.

Old Johnnie Macdonald told me that many years ago. It took him two nights to tell me. I heard him tell it to other people, other children often enough. It was a favourite among some of them . . . but where he'd heard it I couldn't tell you. And he was a great storyteller. It wasn't exactly the story, it was the way he told it – he told it the right Traveller way, so that they could understand it. Old Johnnie, he's gone now, but his stories will live on.

The King and the Lamp

Now, I want to tell you a good story, and I hope you're going to like it. The story is one my daddy used to tell me when I was wee, because I was very fond of a story and I used to say to him, 'Tell us some stories, Daddy!' See, when we were carrying on and being wild Daddy used to say, 'Come on and I'll tell you a story!' So you be quiet, listen. And some day when you're big and have wee babies, you can tell them the same story that I'm telling you!

Many many years ago there was an old tinkerman. And he wandered round the country making tin because in these days everything that we needed was made from tin. And everything he used to make his tin he carried on his back. Some of the tools of his trade were shears for cutting the tin and a soldering bolt for soldering it, and he went from place to place mending pots and kettles, ladles, toasters and all these kinds of things. But unlike any other old Traveller, he was only by himself. He met other Travellers along the way and they wonderd why, but this old man had never got married.

So, one summer he would be in one place, the next summer he would be in another place and the next summer he would be in another – in villages and towns. But there was one particular town he liked better than any other and he always used to come back, every year, because he got a lot of work there. And the funny thing was, something always drew him back – whether it was the town or whether it was because it was close to the king's palace, nobody will ever know.

But one day he landed back. Not far from the town was the palace, it sat up on a great big hill, and in the palace lived the king and the queen. The old man carried his tent on his back as well as his working things, his tools for making tin. He was quite happy when he landed back near the village and he put up his small tent. The next morning he walked into the village. It wasn't very big but he loved this village.

That night he sat up and he worked late, and he made kettles, pots, ladles, spoons – everything that he thought he could make. And the next morning he packed them all on his back and walked into the village. He met a lot of people along the way, people that he had known before and had done some jobs for.

He asked them, 'Have you got anything to mend?'

And they said, 'Yes, we've got things to mend but we just can't afford it.'

'Do you want to buy something then – can I sell you a pot, can I sell you a ladle, can I sell you a toaster?' the tinkerman asked.

But he met the same problem all the way, wherever he went. And the old man began to think, 'Times must be really hard. Nobody seems to want my tinware anymore.' So at last he landed at the end of the village. An old woman lived there and he had known her for years.

He said to her, 'Are your kettles and pots needing mended, my old friend?'

She said, 'Yes, old tinkerman, my kettles and pots need mended.'

'Well,' he said, 'let me do them for you!'

'Well, you can do them for me but I'm sorry I can't pay you.'

'Oh! Why can you no pay me – I'm sure I don't charge you very much for your kettles and pots. Pennies is all, I think.'

She said, 'I couldn't pay you a penny. Old man, I couldn't even pay you a penny.'

'Well, how about a new pan?'

She said, 'My pans are burned through.' (Because tin pans in these days didn't last very long, they were only made of thin tin.) 'We'd love to . . . but everyone here in the whole . . . old man, you'll no sell much here this time.'

'It's been a year since I've been here!'

'But last year was different from this year.'

'But why? Why was last year so different?'

'Well, our taxes have been raised since last year,' she said. 'Our king doesn't give us much chance. And the same thing happens in all the country and all the villages around. The king has made new laws and raised all our taxes. The farmers can't pay them, neither can the villagers pay their taxes to the landlords. And we're so poor that if things don't change, soon everybody'll have to be like you, old Traveller man – we'll have to pack up and go on the road because we can't afford it.'

'Well,' said the old tinker, 'bad business for you is bad business for me. Why doesn't somebody do something about it?'

'What can we do? We can't go to the king and tell him to stop raising our taxes. He takes three-quarters of the corn from the farmers, three-quarters of everything they grow, if they don't have any money to pay his taxes. Then the landlord who we work for does the same with us, and we're so poor we're hardly able to survive.'

'Well,' said the old Traveller man, 'there must be something done about this.'

'Well,' she said, 'there's nobody who can do anything about it. Because we don't want to lose our homes, we don't want to lose our village, we don't want to lose our land – there's nothing we can do.'

So the old Traveller man had tried his best but he never made one single penny that day. He walked home very sad to his own little tent which he had camped outside the village. And he kept in his mind the thought that something had to be done. 'Nobody's going to do it, so,' he said, 'it's up to me. I'll have to do it. Because it's in my interest to do it in the first place.'

Then he lay all night in his bed, his little bed of straw on the ground in his tent. And he thought and he thought and he thought, of a plan to try and help the villagers and the small farmers around the district who were so good to him . . . and then he came up with the answer; the king must be made to understand – and he, a poor tinker, a Traveller tinsmith – he was the very person, the one who was going to make the king understand about the predicament in the village!

The very next morning he got up bright and early, had a little breakfast – which was very meager at this time because he had made no money in the village. He packed his camp on his back, and his tools, and made his way through the village to the king's palace. But he didn't go straight to the palace. On the way from the village there was a road that led up through a forest and then there was a large driveway that led up to a hill, and on the hill was the king's palace.

The story I'm telling you goes back nearly seven to eight hundred years ago. In these days there were lots of trees, hundreds of trees! The whole country was overrun with them. There was more wood than anything else, and the old tinker had little trouble finding a place to put up his tent and sticks for his fire. So where did he choose to put his tent? On the drive going to the king's palace! It was nothing like the drives you have today – it was just a track right through the wood, beautiful and better made than any in the village. In the village they had no roads. But going to the king's palace they had a road made especially for the king's horses and carriages to pass along. The old tinkerman chose a piece of land as close to the palace, as close to the road as he could find, because that's what he wanted to do!

Then he put up his tent and kindled his fire and started to work on his tinware. But he hadn't been working very long, when who came along but the king's caretaker. And he saw the old Traveller man on the pathway.

'Get out of here!' he said. 'Old man, who are you? And what are you doing here?'

The old Traveller man said, 'I'm doing nothing. I am at my work and at my job.'

'But, you can't, man,' he said. 'You can't work and kindle a fire here, this is the king's – the driveway to the king's palace!'

'Well,' the old man said. 'I don't care, the driveway to the king's palace or not. I've pitched my tent here and I'm making my tin here, I've got to make my livelihood.'

So the caretaker who was guarding the palace tried his best to get rid of the old man. But no way, the old man wouldn't move.

'Well,' he said, 'I'll soon find somebody that'll shift you.'

So up the driveway he goes and he sees some of the king's guards. (Now, there were no police in the land in these days, and any soldiers that were available belonged to the king, and the king could command these soldiers to do anything that he wanted.) And the first person that the caretaker of the king's land met was the captain of the king's soldiers.

He said to the caretaker, who was out of breath by this time for he had run nearly a mile and a half, 'Stop, man, what's the trouble!'

He said, 'The trouble' (panting) 'the trouble is – there's an old tinkerman on the driveway leading to the palace. And he's got his fire kindled! He's got his tent there, and he's busy making tinware. And the king is due to go to the village in a very short time!'

'But,' said the king's guard, 'that's no problem. We'll soon square it up.'

He called to five of his troop. They jumped on their horses and rode down the drive. They arrived and the old tinkerman was busy – he had his fire going – working at his tinware.

So the king's officer jumped off his horse along with his soldiers, and commanded the old man to get moving away from the place because the king was due to pass down this way in a very little time.

But the old man said, 'No. I too am a subject of the king. He's my king as well as yours. I don't own any land, I don't have any land, but any land that belongs to the king belongs to me. Because he's my king! And if he's my king and I'm one of his subjects, I'm entitled to park my tent on his land and make my living as well as the next person.'

As he was an old man, the guards did not want to be rough or manhandle him, so they tried to argue with him. They argued and tried to get rid of him when who should appear right at that very moment, but the king in his carriage! Ahead of the coach rode two or three couriers. When the king came to the six horses and his officers standing in the road, he ordered the driver to pull up.

He opened the door of his coach, and said, 'What is the hold-up here?'

And then he saw the fire, he saw the smoke, and he saw the tent of the old man. 'What's going on here?' said the king.

They lowered the steps from the coach and the king stepped down. And he walked out onto the driveway.

The captain of the king's officers bowed to the king and said, 'Your Majesty, we don't want you to see this.'

'Why not?' said the king. 'Why shouldn't I see? Wha-wha-what's going on? What's the trouble here? Why is my driveway . . . I am late as it is, to make an appearance in the village.'

'Well, sir,' he said, 'I've a little explaining to do. It's one of your subjects.'

'One of my subjects? What is the trouble then?'

He said, 'Sir, it's an old tinkerman.'

'An old tinkerman? Well,' he said, 'I'm sure you are a troop of soldiers – I don't think you need to be afraid of an old tinkerman.'

'But, sir, he's got his fire kindled and he's got his tent up and he's making, he's making his livelihood on your driveway!'

'Oh well,' said the king (chuckling), 'that I would love to see! Move – step back!' And the king walked forward.

Sure enough there was the old tinkerman making things he would need to sell. But the thing he was specially making was a lamp – the most beautiful lamp. And he was just about finished with it, when the king stepped forward. And the king was amazed: he saw the common fire, he saw the common tent and he saw a piece of leather laid out, and all the working tools that the old Traveller man had used. The king had never in his life ever seen anything like this! The king had seen lamps and seen kettles, but he had never had an idea where they came from.

So the king was mesmerised and so happy to see this that he told everyone, 'Stay back for a moment, please, just stay back for a moment!'

And everyone had to obey the king. The captain of the guards couldn't do anything. They stood back and held the horses. And the king sat down on his hunkers beside the old man. He watched the old man. The old man paid no attention to the king, never letting on that he knew this was anybody other than a spectator, till he finished the lamp. Then he polished it. And the old man looked up.

He said, 'Your Majesty, will you forgive me?'

The king said, 'Certainly, my old man, I forgive you. But forgive you for what?'

'Well, last night, I was in the village and things were not too good. I had a little money and I went into an ale tavern and I got kind of drunk.' (The old man told him this story.) And he said, 'Eh, with my possessions on my back I wandered here and I wandered there and I didn't know where I was going to find a place to pitch my tent. The only place I could find was here. And I hope you will forgive me, my lord, my king. I didn't know this was the road going to your palace.'

'Oh, come, come, old man, why not? Why not? I'm enjoying this. What is it you're making?'

He said, 'Your Majesty, I am making a lamp. A special lamp.'

The king looked and it really was a special lamp. This old man was a really good tinsmith. He made this lamp and unto his mind he'd made it specially for the king. And no-one could make a better lamp!

The king looked, 'Is it finished?'

And the old man said, 'Yes, my lord, it's finished.'

'Well, you know,' he said, 'my lamps in my palace are not very good and I think that's a better lamp than any I've ever seen. How much would you take for that lamp from me?' said the king.

'Oh! Your Majesty, I would never take anything from you. I just want you not to be angry with me for staying on your ground!'

'Oh no,' said the king, 'I shall not be angry with you, I'm willing to pay you for your lamp. You need to be paid for your lamp! I get paid for everything that I do. Why should you not be paid?'

And the king put his hand into his own pocket and took out four gold crowns and put them in the old man's hand. 'Now,' he said, 'I'm giving you these four gold crowns for your lamp because I want it for myself, for my own room. And I hope that it works. But to be fair on you, if it doesn't work the way I want it to, you're going to be in trouble. So that I can find you again, you stay where you are and don't move! You've got my permission to stay here.'

The king took his lamp in his hand and he walked to his coach, and bade all his soldiers and everybody to go about their business. The king told his footman, 'Drive me on!' He put his lamp in his coach with him. 'That,' he said, 'I'm taking back,' and he waved to the old man through the coach window.

The old tinkerman was quite happy. 'Now,' he said, 'my task is half done.'

So the tinkerman stayed there all that day. The king went about his business, visited the village and did all that he wanted to do, met all the people he wanted to see in the village. And the moment that he returned to his palace in his coach, the first thing he took out with him was his lamp.

Into the palace he went, met his queen who was happy to see him returned, and she said, 'You're home, my lord!'

'Yes,' he said, 'my darling, I'm home.'

'But what is that you have in your hand?'

'Oh, this is something special, my dear. This is a lamp!'

'Oh,' she said, 'I would love to see it working.'

The king said, 'Well, it will be in our bedroom tonight. We will have the most beautiful light that anybody ever had!'

Now, the lamps in these days weren't very popular because you couldn't afford lamps, not the way the old tinker could make them. You had to be very rich to be able to buy a good lamp.

So late that afternoon the king called for the headman in the castle and told him to fill his lamp and have it ready, that he and his queen would have their lamp while they had their evening meal. Now the old tinkerman was in his tent and he kindled his fire, made a little meal to himself, and he just sat back and waited. And he waited. He knew what he was waiting for.

Back in the palace it was evening and all this beautiful food was brought forward to the king and the queen, and placed before them for their supper. But evening in the olden times came very quickly because these old palaces were all built of solid rock and stone, and windows were just barred. So the king and queen were dining and they had a few lights going.

The king said, 'Bring more light! Bring me my lamp, my special lamp that I got this morning as a present from my old friend, the tinkerman. Bring my lamp! And put it beside my meal where I can see what I'm eating!'

Oh, in these days they filled the lamps with tallow, common oil made from melted down animal fat. And they placed what you call 'rushie wicks' in the lamps made from rushes, the insides of rushes plaited together. They didn't have cotton because cotton wasn't invented at that time, so they took the natural wild rushes and split them, took the centres from the rushes and wove them together to make wicks. To make a large flame you would use maybe five, to make a small flame for a night light, maybe one. Or if you wanted a brighter light you used two. So they had special people to make these rushie wicks, not anybody could make one. It could have been a turn for a butler or maybe the cook who made rushie wicks for the lamp. And to make a bright light for their king, the head butler or the head cook had plaited five rushie centres together to make a large wick, and placed it in the king's lamp. And lit it.

The lamp was placed before the king, right beside his supper. The king was delighted because it was blazing and he could see all around him! Shadows had been climbing up the walls; then they disappeared as everything was lit up inside the palace chamber. The king said to himself, 'That is a beautiful lamp. I underpaid the old man who made that lamp for me.'

But as he was eating his supper the funniest thing happened: the tallow in the lamp began to leak out and spread across the table. The king was halfway through his meal when he looked and saw the tallow leaking from the lamp, floating right out over the table. And the light of the flame began to get lower and lower as the tallow escaped – the king looked – the lamp went out.

The king was angry, more than angry, because he had told everyone about his special lamp, then it went out! He was so angry he couldn't eat his supper. And he got so wild he began to shout and walk round the inside of the palace chamber.

'Go!' he said to the captain of the guard. 'And bring me

that old tinkerman here at once. Bring him before me! I'll have his head. I'll have his head for this!'

So naturally, the old tinkerman was waiting. He saw the guards coming. And he knew what was up. They arrested him immediately and fetched him before the king. And he hung his head before the king, right in the king's chamber.

By this time the king's anger had subsided a wee bit. The king was up; he'd only half finished his supper. The queen had retired to her chamber.

'You call yourself a tinsmith?' he said to the old tinker.

'Yes, my lord,' he said, 'my king, I call myself a tinsmith.'

'And,' he said, 'you made the lamp?'

'Yes, my lord,' he said, 'I made the lamp.'

'And you told me that it was the best lamp that you ever made?'

'Yes, my lord,' he said, 'it was the best lamp I ever made. I never made a lamp before like it.'

'And you promised me that it would give me light – better light than any other lamp that you'd ever made?'

'Yes, my lord,' he said, 'I said it would give you better light than any lamp I'd ever made.'

'Well,' said the king, 'look at my table! And I never finished my meal because of your lamp leaking! It destroyed the table, the oil from the lamp destroyed the table and upset me – I never even finished my meal! And you call yourself a tinsmith!'

'Well, Your Majesty, my dear lord, my king, have I your permission to speak in my own way?'

'Yes,' said His Majesty the King, 'you can speak in your own way. And tell me why that lamp is not fit for me!'

'Well, Your Majesty,' he said, 'I work hard, and I made sure that the lamp was fit for you, but it's not my fault.'

'It's not your fault!' said the king. 'Why is it not your fault?
You made it!'

He said, 'Your Majesty, my king, my lord, I made it. But I
couldn't make it any better than I made it. Because if there's
anyone to blame, it's not me. It's the man who gives me the
tin to make my lamp that's at fault, not me. If he'd given me
good tin to make a good lamp for you, my lord, I would
have made a good lamp.'

'Well,' the king said, 'there could be something in that. Go
find the village tinsmith,' he told the captain of the guards,
'and bring him before me this moment!'

Naturally the captain of the guards wasn't long going
to the village and he brought back this tinsmith. And the
tinsmith stood before the king, and he bowed.

The king said, 'You are the tinsmith of the village?'

He said, 'Yes I am. I am the tinsmith of the village.'

'Did you sell this old tinsmith some tin today?'

'Yes,' he said, 'my lord, I sold him some tin.'

'Well,' he said, 'he made me a lamp and the lamp is
hopeless because your tin is hopeless.'

'Well, my lord,' he said, 'if my tin is hopeless it's not my
fault.'

'Why is it not your fault? You are the man who sells the
tin to people who make these things that everyone needs,
and you turn around and tell me that it's not your fault?'

'No, my lord,' he said, 'it's not my fault.'

'Well,' he said, 'whose fault is it?'

He said, 'It's the man from the foundry who produces my
tin that's at fault, not me.'

So the king sent two guards to the smelter in the small
iron foundry who made tin. The man was arrested and
brought to the palace.

Now the old tinker and the tinsmith were sitting there,

and then the man from the foundry who made the tin was called. He was taken before the king and questioned.

His Majesty said, 'Did you sell some tin to the tin dealer who sold this tin to the tinkerman who made my lamp?'

'Yes, my lord,' he said, 'I did. I supply all his tin.'

He said, 'Why is your tin not fit to make a lamp for me?'

'Well, my lord, if the tin's no fit enough, it's not me to blame.'

'Well,' he said, 'who is to blame? Someone has to stand accused for the mistake that was made for me!'

'Well, my lord, it's not my fault.'

'Whose fault is it?' said the king.

He said, 'The fault must lie with the man who makes my bellows to blow my fire to make my heat to make my tin!'

'Well,' said the king, 'fetch him! Bring him here.'

So naturally, off went the king's guards again and brought back the bellows-maker who made the bellows for pumping the air into the fire foundry to melt the ore to make the tin. And he was brought before the king.

The king said, 'Step before me! Bellows-maker, you're charged with . . .' And he told him the whole story as I'm telling you.

The bellows-maker said, 'My lord and my king, you must forgive me! Because—'

'Why should I forgive you? You're the cause of all my trouble, and the trouble of these other men who stand before me – they're condemned! They're going to suffer.'

And the bellows-maker said, 'Well, my lord, my king, it's not my fault.'

'Well,' he said, 'whose fault is it?'

'My lord, it's the man in the tannery's fault, who sells me

my skins to make my bellows.' (Now all these bellows that pumped the fire with air were made from skins.)

The king said, 'Get the man here from the tannery at this moment! I want to get to the end of this. Bring him here before me!'

Naturally, the man from the tannery was sent for, who had tanned all the skins and made the leather that was used in the bellows to blow the fire to melt the ore to make the tin for the old tinkerman. And they were all before the king. So the man from the tannery was brought forward, before the king.

The king accused him straightaway and said, 'Look . . .' and he told him the story I'm telling you. 'You are a man of the tannery?'

'Yes, my lord, I am from the tannery.'

'You make the skins and tan the skins that makes this man's bellows that this man uses to melt this ore to make tin to sell to the tinsmith who sold it to the tinker who made my lamp – and my lamp leaks on my table and upsets my supper?'

'Yes,' says the tanner, 'it's true. But, my lord, it's not my fault.'

'Then, who's at fault?' says the king. 'Someone stands condemned for this thing that's really happened!'

And the man from the tannery said, 'My lord, it's not me. My lord, it's the farmer who sends me the animals, who I get the skins from.'

'Well!' said the king. 'Bring the farmer to me! Immediately. I must get to the end of this, to the bottom of this thing tonight!'

So naturally, the farmer was sent for. And he stood before the king. And the king told him the story I'm telling you.

'You are the farmer,' he said, 'who supplies the skins to the tannery?'

'Yes,' he said, 'my lord, my king, I am.'

'And,' he said, 'the tanner supplies them to the bellows-maker and he sells bellows to the man who melts the ore and the man who melts the ore makes tin to supply tin to the tinsmith and the tinsmith supplies it to this old tinker who made my lamp that destroyed my evening meal?'

'Yes, my lord, that's true.'

'Well,' he said, 'why is it that your skins are not good enough?'

'My lord, and my king,' he said, 'I hope you will forgive me.'

'Forgive you for what? I know I shan't forgive you!' said the king.

He said, 'My lord, there is no-one at fault, if I must tell the truth before my king,' and he bowed. 'Your Majesty, if the skins don't work to make the bellows and the bellows don't work to heat iron and if the iron doesn't work to make the tin and the tin doesn't work well enough to supply the tinsmith who sells it to the old tinkerman to make your lamp, then, my lord, you're at fault!'

'Me,' said the king, 'I am at fault?'

'Yes, my king and my lord, you probably will have my head for this, but I have to tell you – you are at fault.'

'And why,' said the king, 'am I at fault? You mean to tell me I'm at fault for the lamp that I never saw before that spills oil on my table and destroys my evening meal, I'm at fault?'

'Yes, my king,' he said, 'you're at fault.'

'Well, tell me,' he said, 'truthfully, why am I at fault?'

'Well, my lord, to begin with, I grow little grain and three-quarters of that goes to you. With what I've got left I'm not able to feed my animals through the winter. Their skins are so poor that they're not even fit to make a bellows to blow a fire to heat some ore and make some tin to sell to a tinsmith to make a lamp for yourself.'

And the king said, 'Is that the truth?'

'Yes,' he said, 'that's the truth.'

And the king sat back and thought. And he thought for a while.

He turned round and he said, 'Gentlemen, come, gather round, and sit there beside me. You have taught me something that I didn't know. Bring forth the wine!' said the king.

And they brought forth a flagon of wine and he gave every single man a drink.

'Drink to me – but a special drink,' he said. 'I want you to give to the old tinkerman.' And he took his own golden cup, he handed it to the old tinkerman. And the old tinkerman drank half and the king drank the other half.

He said to the old tinkerman, 'You are the one who taught me to be a real king! From now on, no more taxes on the farmers! What they grow they can keep it to themselves, for what good use is it being a king to rule over people who can't even make something for me that I need, because of my own fault!'

And from that day on to this day, the king laid no more taxes on the farmers, and they produced grain and they produced animals and produced skins for the bellows-makers. And the farmers produced the greatest of skins and these great skins were given to the bellows-maker and the bellows-maker made bellows past the common, and these were used in the foundries to blow air into the furnaces to melt iron and the iron was made into beautiful sheets of tin and the beautiful sheets of tin were sold to the tinsmiths, and the tinsmiths made the most beautiful things. And for evermore everyone was happy, except the king – he was left with his lamp that leaked from the old tinkerman!

And that is the last of my story.

The Coal, the Straw and the Bean

It all began a long time ago . . . there once lived a poor old widow-woman, and she lived in a little cottage next to a great farmer. Now this farmer was very rich. He owned the little cottage where the old widow lived, and he charged her money for living there. But the old woman was very, very poor. She had no work; she could not do any spinning or any weaving. She could not do anything, because she was so old and never had any food in her house. She never had any fire in her hearth to heat her. So as the days went into weeks and the weeks went into months, she got poorer and colder and older.

Then one morning she thought to herself, 'I am so hungry, and my fire is out. I have nothing to kindle my fire. I shall go to my neighbouring farmer's field and gather some straws to kindle my fire.'

So she went, and lo and behold it was a field where the farmer had grown all his crop of beans. Now he had collected all his crop and the field was bare. But there were a few straws around that the farmer had missed. And the old woman began to collect them. Oh, and there were a few little beans in the straws! She thought to herself, 'I'll take the beans and have a little meal from them. I'll use the straws to kindle my fire.'

Very carefully she gathered a small armful of straws, picking the ones that the farmer had missed. And who should come along but the rich farmer himself! Now this farmer was very mean. And when he saw the poor old woman collecting the straws in his field he got very upset. He called to the old woman:

'How dare you come to my field and collect the straws!'

And the old woman was very humble. She said, 'I am sorry, sir. But I am so hungry. I am so poor. I don't have any fire. I was wondering if . . . I wasn't doing any harm. I was only collecting the straws you missed from your harvest. They're no good to you, because you will never collect them.'

He said, 'It's my property! You have no right being in there, old woman, in my field!' Oh, he was very angry. So he began to tell the old woman about the way that people should not touch things they don't own and all these kinds of things. When who should come along the road but his neighbour!

Now his neighbour was another farmer. And he had gone off to collect a cart of coal for the fire. When he came along and saw his neighbour the rich farmer arguing with a poor old woman with her arm full of straws, he stopped his horse.

He says, 'What's going on here, neighbour? What's wrong with you? Why are you so angry with the old woman?'

'She's been in my field,' said the rich farmer, 'she's been collecting my straws.'

And the other farmer said, 'Have you not collected your harvest, my friend?'

'Of course, I have. And it's all in the barn set to dry.'

'Then why are condemning a poor old woman for gathering the straws that you left behind? She's not doing any harm. You're not going to collect them, are you?'

'Oh no,' said the rich farmer, 'no way.'

'Well, why do you condemn her?' Then turning to the old woman he said, 'Why are you collecting straws in the field, my dear?'

She said, 'I'm sorry, sir, but I was just collecting them to kindle my fire and pick up a few beans. I have no food in my house and my fire is out. And I am so cold.'

Now this farmer had a large cart of coal that he was bringing back to his farm. Then turning to his neighbour the rich farmer he said, 'Wouldn't it be nice if you could give the old woman something like a sack full of beans – so she could have something to eat?'

'A sackful of beans?' said the farmer. 'Not on your life, my friend! She has no reason to be in my field. I never want to see her in my field again.'

'Well,' said his neighbour, 'can she have the little beans, the little straw that she has collected?'

'Of course she can take them! But she must not come back in my field again!'

'Thank you,' said the poor old woman, 'sir, thank you.'

And then the other farmer said, 'My dear, are you cold? Here is something that will help you,' and reaching into his cart he picked up a big lump of coal. Shiny, black, glossy coal. And he says, 'My dear, with the help of your straws, and if you could find a few pieces of firewood and then you break up this coal, you will have a wonderful fire!' And of course the old woman thanked him very much. The farmer went on his way, and the rich farmer went on his way.

So she took the big lump of coal in her hand and with the little straw she had under her arm she walked back to her little humble cottage.

She began to collect the little beans from the straws and put them in a little pan. Then she began to kindle up the fire with the straws and put some sticks she'd found on the top of the straw, and broke up the big lump of coal that the farmer had given her. Within a few minutes she had a blazing fire going.

'Now,' she said to herself, 'I shall boil my beans that I have collected.' So she took the pan to the fireside.

But unknown to her one single bean had fallen by the hearth of the fire. And while she was kindling the fire, a single straw had fallen. But the old woman paid no attention to that. There by the fireside she was so hungry and so dying for the heat from the coal that she paid no attention to a little bean lying by the fire, and the little straw from the bean field. She boiled the little beans on the fire until they were cooked, and they were ready. She took them to the table, she sat down and ate them up. It was the first meal she'd had for a long, long time. And because she was so heated through by the fire and with her little feast of beans, she fell asleep in her chair.

But by the fireside lay the little bean and the little straw. Then what should fall out of the fire but a burning piece of coal! It landed right beside the straw and the bean. And of course the coal was very annoyed by this.

He said, 'I'm going to go cold.'

And the little bean said, 'I'm going to get very warm.'

And the little straw said, 'I cannot stand the heat! What shall we do?' So the three of them made up their minds – 'Let's run away from this place!'

Meanwhile the old lady is still asleep on her chair by the fireside. She paid no attention to the hot coal from the fire, the straw and the bean. So while the old lady was still asleep, the coal, the straw and the bean made their way from the fireside out through the little kitchen, out the back door. They were going off on a journey. Where they were going no-one was going to know! But they were so pleased because they wouldn't burn by the fireside anymore.

So, the coal, the straw and the bean travelled on. The coal was still glowing hot. The bean was very happy. He had escaped from the pot. And the straw was very happy because he had escaped from the fireside. They travelled on, wondering where they were going to, when they came to a little stream. Now, there's no way a lump of coal is going to cross a little stream because if he fell in, the water would cool him and he would be dead. And of course, if the little bean crossed, he would fall in the water and be gone in the stream.

'What shall we do,' thought the bean, the straw and the coal, 'to cross this little stream?' And then the straw had an idea.

He said, 'Look, my friends, if I were to lay myself across the stream, I could reach from one side to the other. And then you could go across on me. And then I could join you.'

'What a wonderful idea!' said the coal and the bean. 'That's how we'll cross the stream.'

'Then who shall go first?' said the bean.

And the coal said, 'Well, I'm larger than you, so I'll cross first.'

So being a red-hot coal, he crawled across the straw. But because he was so hot, when he came to the middle of the straw, the straw burned through and the coal fell into the stream. With a little sizzle he was gone. Now the straw was broken in two, with the heat of the coal burned through, and he floated away with the stream. And the poor little bean, he's sitting there by the riverside, he watched. He laughed and he laughed so much to see the coal and the straw falling into the river that his belly burst! And he lay there with a burst belly laughing to himself.

And who should come wandering along at that very moment but a tailor! A wandering tailor with his bag of needles and thread on his back, wandering along mending things for people in the towns and farms and houses. And the very first thing he saw when he came to the stream was the little bean lying there with his belly burst. And of course the tailor was very sorry for the little bean.

He said, 'Poor little bean, what's wrong with you?'

But the bean could not speak, for his belly was burst!

'Well,' said the tailor, 'I cannot go on my way and leave you like this.' So he searched his bag for a piece of white thread to sew up the bean. But he searched his bag in vain. There was not a piece of white thread. 'Well, little friend, I want to help you. But the only thing I've got is black thread.' So he took his needle and threaded it through a piece of black thread. Very carefully he sewed the bean's belly up. Then he said, 'I'll say good-bye, my friend, you'll be all right now.' So he walked on his way and left the little bean by the riverside with his belly sewn up with a piece of black thread.

The little bean lay there. He could not move. But he was contented; his belly was sewn up now. He was sorry for the coal, sorry for the straw. But his belly was mended. And he was sorry he had laughed so much to burst his belly in the first place.

But who should come along then but a peddler! A wandering peddler. Now this peddler had been selling things to farmers and people around the villages. He would sell anything! He was about to cross the little stream and he looked down – there he saw a little bean. And he stopped, picked it up.

'Oh, my little bean! You're the strangest bean I've ever seen in all my life. So I'll put you in my bag.' He put the strange little bean in his bag with the black mark on his belly sewed up. And he travelled on.

The first place he came to was a farm.

The farmer said, 'Who are you?'

He said, 'I am a peddler.'

'And what do you peddle?'

So the peddler opened his bag and displayed all the things he was going to sell. And when the farmer saw the bean he picked it up.

He said, 'I have never seen anything like this in all my life – it's a black-bellied bean. I'll buy it from you!'

So the peddler sold the black-bellied bean to the farmer.

The farmer took it, put it in a little pot, he planted it. He grew it, and from that little bean he got many more. Oh, he was so pleased! He was the first man ever to bring a black-bellied bean, to sow it in his field. He grew a large acreage of beans. And people came from all over the land to see the farmer and his black-bellied bean.

So he sold the bean to other farmers, and they grew it, and other people grew it. And soon it became very popular, known to this day as the 'black-bellied bean'!

So now, my children, if you go to your mummy's cereal jar and you look, see a little white bean with a black belly, you will know where it came from – the little tailor's needle a long time ago!

The Hunchback and the Swan

Many years ago there lived an old hunchback, and he was mute – he could hear but he couldn't utter a word. He lived in the forest by himself and he had nobody, no friends or relations. And he used to make his living by gathering sticks in the forest, cutting them up into firewood, taking them into the village and selling them to the local inhabitants. Everybody liked to buy the sticks from the hunchback, but they really hated him because he was so ugly – he had a hump on his back, his face was long and his chin was long, and he had so ugly an appearance – just to look at him kind of frightened you! And when he went to the village to sell his sticks the children used to shout and call him names. It made him so sad. And he couldn't get his sticks sold fast enough so he could get back home to his little hut he had built in the forest.

But unknown to the local inhabitants, he had more friends than anybody could ever ask for: he had friends in the forest – the birds, the mice, rats, squirrels, rabbits – all the little people of the forest. The squirrels would come, they would sit on his knee and take things out of his hand. Dormice, rats and rabbits, they loved him dearly and he loved them.

Many's the day he used to walk into the middle of the forest where a wee lake was, and on this lake there lived one

Swan, a Mute Swan. And unlike the whooper swan, it was there all summer and winter as well.

But good as the hunchback was to all these little animals, one he could never get to come near him was the Swan. And he loved and adored it. Once he had sold all his sticks, had come back and fed all his little animals, after they had all come round about him, he would take up a wee bit sandwich or a piece and make his way to the lake in the forest. He would sit by the lakeside, sit and admire the Swan. Time passed by.

It came summer again. The hunchback made his way back to the lake and he took some of his pieces and some food with him and cast all these bits of bread into the water. But the Swan wouldn't come near him. Day out and day in the robin would come and sit on his shoulder, the squirrel would come and sit on his knee, the dormouse, the rabbits and the rats, even the deer, would gather round him. And he would pet them, give them his time. But in his heart he only lived for one thing, the Swan. He admired this Swan, this most beautiful Swan – its long graceful neck and its wings and its feet as it sailed round the lake. But it would never come near him! Day out and day in he pined for the Swan . . . threw pieces in the water, cast them as far as he could, see if he could entice it near him . . . and he had the power upon all animals! But he had no power upon the Swan. It seemed to ignore him completely; it never had any time for him.

But this didn't stop him: day out and day in he cut his sticks, went to the village, sold his sticks to the people, and they gave him just enough money so he could buy whatever he needed in the shop, just enough to keep him alive. Then back he would come, home again, set sail and try, sit by the lakeside and cast his bread upon the water, see if he could feed the Swan – but no. In vain. Could he entice the Swan? No way could he entice it to come near him. Till day passed and day passed and the summer was beginning to end.

Now the summer passed away and October came in. The cold bite of the winter wind began to blow through the forest and all the little animals began to think the winter was coming in. The dormouse started to build up his little bit of stores and the robins began to choose their bits of territory where they were going to spend the winter, the hedgehog looked for a place to curl up and the deer began to grow their coats of long hair. All the animals began to see that winter was coming.

But the hunchback still went to the lake. And the Swan still sailed round. Not a sound came from the Swan because it was mute. And as the days grew shorter, the more the hunchback became in love with the Swan. Till one morning.

The people in the village were waiting on their sticks – the hunchback never turned up. Now these people depended on the hunchback every day. But for a second day the hunchback never turned up, and for a third. The people in the village who really hated him, and even the children who used to shout names at him and call 'Hunchback!' said, 'Oh, the hunchback never turned up today.' They began to miss him.

But he wasn't missed as much in the village (the people only missed him because they had nothing for their fire) as he was in the forest. The robin and the sparrow and the shelfie and the blackbird, and the deer and the rabbits, and the vole and the hedgehog – all began to wonder what had happened to their wee friend. He never put in an appearance and he had always used to, every day. Even the Swan, who evaded him so much, began to turn round in the lake in circles and wonder – she had spied him many times and she wanted to come, but something kept her back, something kept her apart because she was a Mute Swan. Till the third day passed and all the animals in the forest began to wonder why their little friend didn't come and feed them and play with them, come and see them!

And the squirrel went to the robin and the robin went to the blackbird, and the blackbird went to the mavis and the mavis went to the shelfie and they all gathered together. They were a-chirping and a-singing and a-singing and a-chirping in the forest, wondering what had happened to their friend the hunchback. They were going to have a meeting to see what was wrong. So, the robin – he was the master of the lot because he is the master of winter – gathered them round. There were the deer, the rabbits, there were the hares, there was the hedgehog, the squirrel, and even the pine marten was there! The rats and every little creature in the forest gathered into a circle. Everyone was worried.

And the robin spoke up. 'Ladies and gentlemen,' he said, 'I know we're gathered here today in the forest and it's a sad thing we have to talk about. Our little friend who comes and visits us and who's been so good to us every day, there's something wrong because he's never put in an appearance for three days. We must find out what's wrong!'

So the little squirrel, he was very clever, he says, 'Well, Robin, you've chosen yourself to be spokesman for the crowd – what do you think we should do?'

And the robin said, 'Well, there's only one thing we can do, we must find out what is wrong with the hunchback!'

'But how,' Squirrel said, 'are we going to find out what's wrong with him? His house is shut, the windows are closed, the door is locked, there's no smoke coming from his chimney, and we can't go into his place. What can we do? We know there's something wrong.'

'Well,' said the robin, 'there's only one thing we can do, we'll go and see Mister Owl and he'll tell us what's wrong.'

So all the wee animals forgot about being bad to each other – they all went together to the old hollow oak tree. There sitting in the tree was Mister Owl. So they told him their story.

And the owl said, 'Yes, I believe it,' and he listened to what they had to say.

'Well,' Mister Owl said, 'ladies and gentlemen and little friends, I know we are here today, and we're all enemies and we're all friends. But the dearest friend we have is ill. And there's something we must do about it.'

So the robin said, 'Mister Owl, tell us what we've got to do! We know we miss him and we love him dearly. We know he's not missed in the village, they'll only miss his firewood. But we can't live without him! What can we do?'

'Well,' says the owl, 'you, Mister Robin, being spokesman for the crowd, the only thing you can go and do – we must get a message to our lady, send a message to our lady and tell her! I have seen him and he comes every day, he sits by the lakeside and tries his best to encourage our lady to come and see him! But she never pays any attention to him. I've watched him,' said the owl, 'from my tree up here, watched him coming day out and day in trying to entice her with pieces and everything you could ask for. He is in love with our Lady of the Lake and she doesn't want anything to do with him!'

So all the little creatures gathered round together, they hummed and hawed, disputed and talked about it to each other. They said, 'Well, Mister Owl, what is it we can do?'

'Well, the only thing,' the owl said, 'we can do is send a message and tell her that she is hurting us and disturbing us by being unkind to our little friend! Can she come and see him, so he will know that everything's all right? Probably it will make him well again.'

'But,' the robin said, 'I can't go out into the lake, fly out there and tell her!'

'Aha,' said the owl, 'that's no trouble! Call on our friend Mister Swallow. He is the man that can deliver any message, all over the world he can deliver messages!'

So they called on the swallow. He came in and they told him the story. 'Swallow,' they said, 'would you be kind enough to go out to the Lady in the Lake, our dearest lady whom we all love and admire, and tell her the story we're going to tell you: our little friend, the hunchback, whom we love and admire and adore, is ill in his little cabin in the forest, is ill and sick? And there's nothing we can do to help him – that she is the only one who can come and help him!'

'Gladly!' said the swallow. 'I'll gladly do that because he also is good to me. I enjoy his company. Many's the time he sits in the forest – not that I eat the food that he gives me – but I like the company he has around him.' And just like that – away goes the swallow.

The swallow flies out into the middle of the lake and he hovers above the Swan. Now all the little creatures of the forest were sitting on the bank of the wee lake and they were waiting to see what happens. So the swallow stops, and while he circles he tells her the story. Then the swallow circles round and comes back. They all wait and wait and wait . . . and the Swan turns. She begins to swim towards the bank. When all the other creatures see the Swan swimming towards the bank they begin to feel happy! They know now that the Swan has received the message and she's going to do something about it.

So the Swan comes in, steps up onto the shore and makes

her way up the wee path to the forest. Step by step goes the Swan, step by step right to the hunchback's cabin, pushes the door with her beak and the door opens.

And all the little creatures of the forest gather round! There's some trying to keek through the windows. Inside the hunchback is lying on his back, quiet and still, not a movement from him lying still on his bed. As ugly as sin. And the robin goes to the window – he's the only one that can fly up to the window – and all the other little creatures are sitting on the ground.

And they're shouting up to him, 'What is she doing now?'

And the robin's flying up, flapping at the window (he couldn't stop, you see), shouting back to them, 'She's coming through the door!'

'What else, Robin?'

'She's walking up to his bed.' He's broadcasting what the Swan's doing back to all the other creatures. Now the squirrel, the hedgehog, the rabbit – they're all gathered round the wee cabin.

So the Swan walks up to the bed and she looks. There's the hunchback lying on his back, pale as could be, ugly as sin. Sick as could be. And the Swan looks and the Swan feels sad. She thinks back. 'How often I've seen him sitting on the bank casting the bits of pieces on the water for me to get. He could never hurt me,' she said to herself. 'He never meant to hurt me in any way. Why is it that I thought so often he would do me an injury?' And the Swan goes up.

She reaches her neck across his neck – her long slender neck that the hunchback loved so much – and she lays it across the hunchback's. The minute she did that the hunchback opened his eyes and he looked – he saw the Swan. And he put his hands around the Swan's neck.

The robin says, 'The Swan has finally accepted him! And he's cuddling the Swan.' He's passing the words back to the wee animals all round the cabin.

And they say, 'He cuddles the Swan, he cuddles the Swan, the Swan is accepting him! Our lady, our lady's accepting him! Now perhaps he will be well!'

After the hunchback opens his eyes, sees the Swan and pets her neck, he sits up in bed and says to himself, 'It feels so good . . .'

But all in a minute the Swan turns round her beak and picks a feather from her wing and holds it up . . . she takes it and pierces it into the hunchback's chest. And an amazing thing happens – the hunchback's ugliness begins to disappear, his body stretches . . . and he turns into a Swan!

The robin's watching at the window and all the wee animals said, 'What's happening now, what happened? Tell us what's happening now, tell us what's happened!'

The robin's breast was so full that a lump came in his throat. The robin couldn't speak because he was so happy. He couldn't say a word but only twittered. And he sat down. All the animals asked him to speak up and tell them what was going on, but the robin couldn't speak or say another word, he was so full.

Then, all the animals gathered round the front door and the next thing they saw was *two* Swans walking out the cabin door, one after the other. The one followed the other to the lake. And in the lake they went sailing away. All the animals gathered round.

They said, 'At last our little friend is happy.'

But the robin couldn't speak. From that day on to this day the robin only repeated himself; he's never said another thing.

So the two Swans dwelt in the lake and the animals said, 'Our lady has finally found a friend.'

And from that day to this, the Swan utters nothing. That is the story of the Mute Swan – the way it was told to me is the way I'm telling you. And that's the last of my wee story.

Now that is an old, old story, told to me many, many years ago by an old uncle of mine who really was a great storyteller. He wandered all over Scotland by himself for years and years. He was a piper and played his bagpipes for a living. In the wintertime he would have settled in some Traveller community, played his bagpipes to them, spent his time with them and picked up all their stories. He travelled in the summertime but as he had been born and reared in Argyllshire, he often returned there and spent the winter with his sister who was my mother. On the winter nights in my time there was no television or no wireless, and my uncle, to keep us quiet, would tell us a story and this was one of the stories he told us. Hector Kelby, an Aberdeenshire Traveller, also told me a version of 'The Hunchback and the Swan', on Braemar Green in 1948, while we were waiting for the start of the Highland Games.

The Two Trees

Some years ago in a forest in the north of Scotland there lived an old forester. He had a little cottage nearby but he tended the local forest, cut all the dead branches and dead trees, stored them up and packed them aside. He'd keep the forest clear, and would look after that wood like he looked after his own family. There were oak trees, birch trees, all types of trees in the forest. He loved that forest, and every time he'd see a little bit of clearing that was kind of bare in the forest, if he found a sapling, he would plant it there and watch it grow. He loved that place. Till one morning after he said good-bye to his wife to continue his work he walked towards the forest.

And on the way to the forest along a narrow channel that led to the wood there was a deep ditch. He had cleaned that ditch many times to let the water run by. He stopped for some reason and looked, saw two little saplings growing by the side of the banking of the ditch. And he looked down.

He said, 'There's no point in you growing there, little friends. Let me take you . . .' And very carefully he took his knife, cut the earth right around the little saplings and picked them out, cut them out. They were about six inches long. He carried them into a clearing in the middle of the forest beside a big giant oak tree, King of the Forest. And he planted these two little saplings, dug a hole with his knife, planted them very carefully. He knew they would grow – apart from each other.

But unknown to the forester one of them was a silver birch and the other a willow, a little willow tree. So the two trees took root and began to grow. And of course birch trees grow quickly, very fast. Within four or five years the birch was a beautiful young sapling growing up into the air, a silver birch. The other one, a little bush, was a willow. It never grew very much. It spread its little branches out but never grew any higher. But because it didn't grow up, it was very jealous – jealous of the little Lady of the Forest, the silver birch tree. And in all its spare time the willow kept nattering and nagging at the birch tree.

'Oh, you think you're beautiful, don't you!' it said. You think you're wonderful, you think you're the Lady of the Forest! Well, let me tell you something: some day the woodcutter will come and they'll cut you down, take you away; they'll cut you in pieces and use you for many purposes. But they won't touch me because I'm no good to them anyway.' And so it bickered nonstop, day out and day in.

And of course in the dark sided forest where there was no one around, the local trees began to get annoyed at this. So they had no option. They told their king, the King of the Forest, the great oak, something would have to be done about this. And the King of the Forest didn't want to annoy his friends, the trees.

And he said, 'Well we've got to find peace, no matter what it costs, we'll have to have peace in the forest.' So he told his friend the North Wind the story I'm telling you.

And the North Wind said, 'What would you like me to do, my king?'

And the old King of the Forest said, 'There's only one option – blow her down! Get rid of her.'

So the next time he blew through the forest he blew so hard when he came to the little clearing, he blew the silver birch, the Lady of the Forest down, and she fell with a crash. And the next day when the foresters and woodcutters came through the forest to see the damage that had been done with the storm, they were very sad to see the beautiful silver birch tree blown down with the wind. So they had no option. They took her and cut her up, carried her away and cleaned all the branches off. And there, left by herself, was the little willow bush.

At last it was gone . . . now she had nobody to talk to.

The trees in the forest hated her now for what she had done, unknown to the humans. No one would talk to the willow, no one would listen to her. She had no one to speak to, no one to argue with. And so she began to get very, very sad and her little branches began to bend and lean, in sorrow for what she had done. Her friend that she had liked in her own way, the only company she had, was gone. She worried. And sometimes she cried. And the most amazing thing was, when some of the woodcutters passed through, and even the forester himself when he passed by the bush in the clearing in the morning, in the Spring morning he would look – every little piece of the bush was hung with little dew drops. And when he looked at it he would think it was crying. And maybe it was. Maybe it was crying for the loss of its friend. We'll never know.

And it was the old forester himself who said, when someone mentioned it, 'It looks to me like a weeping willow.'

And so to this day, if you see a willow with its branches bending downwards instead of upwards, it's called a weeping willow. That's why it's weeping today, still, for the loss of its little friend who it had argued with so much in the forest a long time ago.

The old Travellers used to go at night-time away back in time and choose the silver birch, because there were some of them very good at making clog soles. And because beech was too hard, not easy carved, the Travellers used to get the birch trees. They would go at night with their little saw, cut down a birch tree and then cut it in chunks, cut bark off the outside and split them down the middle. And then they would go to the cobbler; he would ask for a dozen of fours, a dozen of five, six inches, sevens, clog soles of the birch. And they would sell them to the cobbler. He would tap the leather on to make clogs. All clog soles are made of wood, and the most famous of all was birch, because it was soft, easy carved and dried fast. People liked it; it was very light when dried and easy on the foot.

In the spring Travellers collected birch tops, which they sold to whisky distilleries, used to give the brew a colour. And witches made their brew from birch!

Archie's Besom

Many years ago on the west coast of Argyll there lived two
brothers called Alex and Archie. They had a small croft and
also did odd jobs apart from their own farm work. Archie
had never married and Alex had lost his wife, so the two
of them just stayed with each other. But Archie being the
youngest brother, Alex would always be the master for the
whole time, and he made his brother Archie work for him
for most of his life. He never paid him a full week's wage,
only a sixpence now and again when he thought that he
should give him something. And Archie was quite content
to work away with his brother because he never knew any
better. He had his food and his clothes, his bed, he had
nothing else and he always had his brother for company.
They shared this little croft between them and the biggest
job they did was building drystone dykes for other farmers
in the district. They also had to take on contracts of building
sheep dykes, fanks for keeping the sheep in made of stone.

One day Alex and Archie were out on the hillside building
this dyke between them. Now this hill they were on, there
was a road leading over that took you down into the village,
and they were busy working away. It was a nice summer's
day when along the road came a tinkerman. He stopped
when he saw the two brothers building this dyke because it
was close to the road. And he asked them for a match.

Alex said, 'Sure, I will give you a match.' He put his hand in his pocket, took out the box of matches and gave him some.

The tinkerman said to the two brothers, 'Is this your ground here you are working on?'

'No,' Alex said, 'it is not wir ground. Why do you want to know?'

'Well,' he said, 'I want to know if I could have some of that heather, that fine carlin heather?'

And Alex said, 'Och sure! The farmer wouldnae object to ye having some of his heather. What are you going to do with it anyway?'

'Well, I make besoms, heather besoms for sweeping the houses out and sweeping the doors and driveways and that.'

'Och,' Alex says, 'I know what besoms are; so ye're a besom maker?'

'Yes, I make besoms.'

So Archie spoke up, 'What do ye get for these besoms ye make?'

'Well, it is a good business – I get a sixpence. Sometimes if it is a better one and I am in a good mood I get a shilling.'

'O-o-och,' says Archie, 'that's a lot of money! A shilling!'

The tinkerman says, 'It is not much money when you consider you have to work nearly a couple of hours to make a besom.'

Archie says, 'You mean to say you can make a sixpence in a couple of hours?'

'Well,' says the tinkerman, 'it takes me about that long to make a really good besom.'

'And you make it with that heather there?'

'Yes, with the heather.'

'Well,' Archie says, 'go ahead and help yirsel to that heather!'

So the tinkerman jumped over the dyke and started pulling the heather. Archie put down his tools for working on the dyke, went over and stood beside the tinkerman. He watched him working the heather. The tinkerman was pulling the longest, finest, straight carlin heather he could get and making it into a big heap to carry under his arm. When he had what he thought would be enough to make two or three besoms, he jumped over the dyke again.

He was just about to go away, when Archie followed up a wee bit by the road and said, 'Is it hard to make these besoms?'

The tinker said, 'No, they're not really hard to make. You tie them up with a piece of rope or a string and just work them round tight. Get a good strong brush handle or a bit of hazel for a stick; just tie them on to the stick, cut off the points and give them a good scrape with a sharp knife – make yourself a good besom!'

'Oh aye,' Archie said, 'that's how ye do it!' He thanked him very much, and away the tinker went.

So he walks back to his brother and Alex says, 'Come on, come on, Archie, let's get finished with this work!'

Archie says, 'No, Brother, I am not doing any more work for you.'

'What do you mean, you are not doing any more work for me?'

'Well,' he says, 'it is just this way: that tinkerman comes along there and pulls some heather from the back of the dyke and makes besoms; he goes and sells them for a shilling or a sixpence, which is a lot of money; and I work with you lifting these stones, building these dykes and sorting roads, digging ditches, doing all the kinds of work round the place and all you give me is a sixpence for a week!'

'But,' says his brother, 'I give you your food and your clothes and your shelter.'

'But you are my brother and my father left the place to us both; I am entitled to as much of it as you are!'

And Alex says, 'Well, I suppose that is right. But you know I need you to help me.'

'Well, you are getting no more help from me to build any more dykes!'

Alex says, 'You will have to do something to keep yourself alive. How are you going to get any money?'

'I am going to make besoms,' he says, 'the same as the tinkerman does. And I am going to sell them.'

But Alex says, 'Archie, you can't make any besoms – you are not a tinker! These are craftsmen, these people know what they are doing, they know the trade and know how to sell them. You have never done that before in your life; you can't make a besom, or couldn't sell it suppose you made one!'

But Archie says, 'I could try, couldn't I? So you mightnae say any more, Brother! I'm not doing any more work,' and he jumped over the dyke. Over he goes and starts pulling the heather. He pulled and he pulled – twice as much as the tinkerman pulled – but by the time he was finished it was nearly stopping time. So the two of them walked home to their small croft and Archie carefully carried his heather, put it in the byre and went in and had his supper.

'Well,' he said, 'I had better go and get started to my work.' Out he goes and takes a brush, cuts the handle off Alex's byre brush, goes in, gets a nice piece of strong copper wire and gets all his heather, makes it into a bundle and ties it onto the stick – makes what he thought looked like a besom, the ones he'd seen before. He tied it tight, as much as could, cut the points off with a sharp knife; and then tried to sweep up. But it was that heavy he could barely lift it. So he carried it in, took it to his brother. He said, 'Alex, now what do you think of that?'

'Och,' Alex says, 'th-that's a terrible besom!'

'What do you mean, it's a terrible besom? That's a good besom!'

He said, 'No-one will buy that from you: it is far too big, there's no-one can handle that. That's not a besom at all! I'll bet you it is not something like what the tinker makes.'

'Well, I don't know,' he said, 'if it is something like what the tinker makes or not, but tomorrow morning I am going to sell it. And if I can't get a shilling for it, I will get a sixpence – I won't need to work a week for it!'

So after breakfast next morning, true to his word, Archie gets the besom on his back, says good morning to his brother Alex and away he goes down the road.

'Och,' Alex shakes his head after him, 'he will be back sadder and wiser.'

When Archie travels on there are a lot of small houses and crofts and farms along the way but every one off the road. No-one would look at the besom. Some would say it was too big or they would have bought it if it was better or they got one from a tinkerman just the day before. But Archie harped all day till he travelled further than he had ever been before. (In these days the crofters never travelled far except when they went for a day at the market.)

At the last house he looked and saw a path going up the hill. 'There is a wee cottage on the top of the hill,' he says. 'Probably the tinker never went there, too far off the road for him by the time he had hawked these cottages. Maybe I will go up there and maybe I will sell my besom.'

So he walks up this crooked path right to this house at

the top of the hill. He knocks at the door and waits a while. He knocks again. Then a woman comes out to him – the fattest woman that Archie had ever seen in his life! She was as broad as she was long, but she had the most happy face on her that Archie had ever seen.

'Hello, my man!' she said. 'What can I do for ye?'

Archie said, 'Well, ma'am, to tell you the truth, you could help me.'

'Well, how could I help?' And he has got this thing on his back – she is standing inside the door and can only see the handle – the top of the besom on his shoulder is so high it's stuck up above the door.

He says, 'I've come to sell ye a besom.'

She says, 'What did you say?'

'I've come to sell ye a besom!'

'Oh, it is the very thing I could do with, a besom! Is it a big one or a small one?'

'Well, I don't know if it is a big one or a small one, but it is kind o' large.'

She says, 'Can you let me see it?' So Archie took it off his shoulder, took it in and put it down in front of her. When she looked at this besom her eyes just lighted up. 'Yes, I'll buy yir besom. I definitely will buy yir besom! How much do you want for it?'

'Well, it took me a while to make and I am not so good at making them as I am only learning . . . I think a sixpence would be enough money.'

'I'll take yir besom,' she says, 'and I am going to give you a sixpence! But this sixpence is a magic one and every time you spend it there is always another one will take its place.'

'Och away,' he says, 'ye're kidding me in, ye're pulling my leg!'

'No, I'm not pulling your leg,' she says. 'You take that

sixpence and you will never need to want for the rest of your days!' So she gave it to Archie and he was quite happy.

He travels back the road to his brother's singing to himself all the way. There we leave Archie to carry on, make the rest of his besoms.

But unknown to Archie, this old fat woman in this cottage was a witch, a witch so big and fat that all the other witches hated her. She could never get a broom big enough to carry her till the day that Archie came to her door with this big besom! So she cackled to herself when Archie had gone, took it in the house and put a magic spell on it. She put it between her legs and tried it around the room . . . 'Just the ideal thing,' she says to herself. 'This is the very thing for me!'

Now all the witches in the district were having a meeting miles away in this wood. It was a birch wood because witches always like to have meetings there, and they landed in one of the clearings.

When everyone had landed they all cackled to each other, 'Ha-ha, she will not be here tonight.' They were referring to Maggie, Fat Maggie, because they thought she couldnae get a besom to carry her to the meeting. Anyway, they didnae want her there because she was too strong and too powerful for them.

But they were just beginning – when Fat Maggie got Archie's besom between her legs – out through the door and away she went right through the air as fast as she could go, landed right in the centre of the circle, in the middle of the wood among them all! They got such a surprise to see her with this large besom, with her sitting on it.

'Ha-ha!' she said. 'You thought that I wouldnae get here! But I'm Fat Maggie, the fat witch that none of you likes when you are going to have a meeting . . . Well, tonight I am going to sit in the meeting and everyone will do what I tell you to do! And when the meeting is finished I'm the only one that is going to be able to fly home!' Like *that* – she went round everyone and took every one of their besoms, threw them right up into the trees – they were stuck in the birch trees.

So after the meeting Maggie took her besom and flew home, put it behind the door happy and contented. And the rest of the witches had to walk all the way for miles and miles back to their own places.

But to this day, if you are walking through a birch wood and you look up, you'll see these things sticking in them you might mistake for crows' nests, but they are not. They are what you call 'witches' brooms' – these are the legends of the brooms that Fat Maggie had flung up into the birch trees.

And that is the end of the story.

This is a story I never heard from a Traveller, but from a man in Argyll when I was young; the brother of a crofter, Neil McCallum, a Gael, a fine speaker of Gaelic and a great storyteller. He and I used to work together on drystone dykes back in Argyll, where he told me many fine tales.

True and Untrue

Once upon a time a long, long time ago, away in this country there was a wee village. And in this village lived an old man who had two sons. Because one son never told any lies in his life, and he couldn't do anything bad, the old man called him True. And the other one told that many lies, did that many bad things, the old man cried him Untrue. They stayed with their father in this wee house in the village. So, one day the old man called the two boys in to him.

'Well, True,' he said, 'I've looked after you well since your mother died, and that's been a long time now. You are old enough now I think to look after yourself. So, there's not much about this wee croft that'll keep the three of us working, not that I'm chasing you away, but do you think that maybe you could go away out to the country and look for a job to yourself?'

'Well,' says True, a good laddie, 'Father, to tell you the truth I was just thinking the same thing myself. I know you brought me and my brother up and looked after us well since my mother died, and did the best for us. We'd like to repay you in some way for what you've done for us.'

'Ah, never mind that,' said the father, 'you don't need to repay me for anything. You're my laddies. And you, True, have been a good laddie to me.'

So, in comes Untrue. 'Look, Untrue,' the father says, 'your

brother was thinking of going away to the country and looking for a job to himself. So, I think you wouldn't be doing any harm if you went with him and kept him company, looked after him. I took care of you well, and for all I've got here I can manage myself now. Not that I'm chasing you away!'

'No,' says Untrue, 'it doesn't matter anyway, suppose you chase me away; I'm getting kind of fed up here anyway.' He wasn't a very good one.

So, before they left, their old father said to them, 'Look, boys, you'll need to take something with you to eat along the way, it'll help you.'

'Ah no,' says Untrue, 'I can't be bothered carrying anything on my back. What am I going to carry food for? I'll get food wherever I go.'

True says to his father, 'Father, you can give me something, I'll carry it.'

So, True packed his bag, took whatever he could get, put it on his back and carried it. Away the two of them go.

Now they wandered down this country road, oh, miles here and miles there and they came to this forest. And it came night-time. True kindled a wee fire and cooked whatever his father had given him to eat.

Untrue says, 'Come on, give me some of that to eat!'

'But,' says True, 'my father offered you whatever you wanted, as much as you could take with you, bacon to roast and oatmeal bannocks, things like that. You were too lazy to carry it. And you expect me to give you half of what I've got?'

'Ah well,' says Untrue, 'I'm your brother!'

Says True, 'I'll give you a wee drop* of it, but I'm not giving you it all.' So, True shared as much as he could give him; but that wouldn't please Untrue.

* wee drop – small amount

'Ah,' he said, 'you're keeping all that you've got to yourself – you're keeping too much to yourself – you're not sharing with me at all!' So, he jumped on top of his brother and pulled a blazing stick out of the fire, rammed it into his brother's two eyes, and blinded him for life! Untrue took all the food, ate everything himself, then cleared out and left his brother in the forest.

Now poor True, he's alone and doesn't know what to do. He's blind and bumping into stumps here, bumping into bushes there and he says, 'Lord bless me, what's going to happen to me? That brother of mine's blinded my eyes for life!' He was in an awful state. But he bumped into this big tree and the branches were low down. He groped round them. And he knew by the quietness – he couldn't see – but he knew by the quietness it must be near midnight. He was in awful pain but he climbed up the tree.

'I can't wander through the forest at night,' he said, 'because I might fall over some precipice and be killed, or something might happen to me. It's bad enough not being able to see, but it's worse to fall over some cliff and lie with broken legs or broken arms and not move till you die!' But he climbed up this tree and sat on a big branch.

It was lucky for him it was the first day in May, when all the wee animals in the woods and forest gathered together below this tree. There was a wolf, foxes, rabbits, stoats, weasels, mice, rats, all gathered under this tree, because on the First of May they were all friendly with each other; there was peace among them all for one day only. They all came here to tell their stories and things, all the secrets that they knew. Well, True didn't know this. So, he's sitting on this branch and hears all these wee voices down below the tree.

And the first to speak up was the hare, the spokesman for them all:

'Well, once more it's come around again, animals, the First day in May is this morning. And as youse know for one whole day all the animals of the forest will be able to speak. All the animals in the forest will be friendly with each other; there will be no fighting, no quarrels, no nothing! The weasel won't chase the rabbit or the fox won't chase the rabbit, or the wolf won't chase the fox. Nothing will touch nothing else; for one day we must all have peace in the forest.'

'All right,' say the rest of the animals, 'we all agree.' This is what they did every year.

'But before we go any further,' he said, 'who has got the most secrets?'

Up spoke the fox. 'Me!' he said. 'I think I'm about the cutest of the lot of youse, I think I've got the most secrets.'

'Well,' said the rest of the animals; and up spoke the rat, 'Okay then, tell us your secrets!'

'The secrets I'm going to tell this morning,' he said, 'are the secrets that a lot of people, these human beings, would like to know, because they'll never know. And they'll never know by me!'

'Well,' said the rest of them, 'let's hear it – if it's a story or something, let's hear it!'

He said, 'It concerns a king.'

Said the little animals, 'We're interested, let's hear it!'

'It concerns a king not very far from here who's got a great big castle, and he's blind. He would give any man a great fortune who could make him see again. Ah, I know how to make him see, but he'll never know by me!' So, the rest of the animals are getting really interested, all sitting round in a ring with their ears cocked up and the fox is talking to them all, see!

'Ah, Fox,' they said, 'don't leave us like that, tell us the rest! We would like to hear, how could a blind king get his eyesight back?'

'Ah, if he only knew,' said the fox, 'the happy man he would be!'

'What would he need to do,' says the hare, 'to get his eyesight back? Say it happened to one o' us, what would we dae?'

'Oh,' he said, 'we could do the same thing.'

'Well,' he says, 'tell us! Because it could happen to us: we could run into a bush, run into a thorn. Me myself, I'm always stotting through thorns and bushes. If I get blinded what would I do?'

'Well,' says the fox, 'all you need to do, the First day of May, go to a wee buttercup and take a dewdrop, squeeze it into your eye. Then you'd see again, on the First of May!'

'Very good,' say the rest of them, 'that is very good. You are a clever fox.'

'That's not bad,' says the wolf, 'not bad at all. But I know a better one than that.'

'Nah,' Fox says, 'you don't know a better one than that – I'm flyer than you, Wolf, you don't know!'

'Ah, but I do! You're talking about your king. But in a land not far away from here,' he said, 'I know a town and a village, and in that village is a well, a bubbling crystal well. And that water in that well can cure anything, anything at all. If I was dying of any kind of disease, if I had the mange, my hair was falling out or I had any kind of trouble, broken legs or broken arms; all I'd need to do is go to that well, duck myself into it or take a wee drop of its water and I'd be as right as rain once more.'

'Ah, come on, come on,' says the rabbit, 'tell us more! It could happen to me: I could take a disease or something and I would be needing to get cured. What was I going to do?'

He says, 'You couldn't do it; these humans can do it, but they'll never know by me!'

'But,' Rabbit says, 'why has the well cured so many folk before; why can it not cure them now?'

'They don't know,' Wolf said, 'in below the stepping stone of the well sits a big black bullfrog. It's him that's keeping the water from curing the folk; if they would take him out and kill him, once more the crystal water would cure them all and there would never need to be any more trouble in the village.'

Now True is sitting up the tree listening to this! He never heard anything like this before in his life. He says to himself, 'If only I could see; if they're telling the truth a happy man I'll be.'

But next who spoke up was the hedgehog, 'Ach, that's nothing!'

'What have you got to say, Hedgie?' says the fox.

'Well,' he said, 'you know what like I am; I'm always wandering into folk's gardens and wandering here and there. I overheard something said, and they humans don't know what it's about.'

'Well, come on, come on, come on,' says the hare, 'tell us about it!'

'It's like this,' he said. 'In a village not far away from here they have a tree. And this tree used to grow lovely beautiful fruit. Oh, it was magical fruit, the greatest in the world, the Fruit of Happiness. If you went under the tree and you were sad, down and broken-hearted, all you would need do was get a wee bit of this fruit of this tree. It made you happy as happy could be, happy as ever! But now there's no more fruit on the tree.'

'Ah, come on,' says the wolf, 'come on, you're not going to stop there, tell us the rest! What would happen to me – I could be out and something goes wrong, I could be sad and not know what to do with myself – and I don't like being sad. What would I do?'

'Ah,' he said, 'there's nothing you could do; but there's something these humans could do, if they only knew.'

'Well,' said the hare, 'what stopped the fruit from being so good as that, the Fruit of Happiness?'

'I'll tell you,' he said. 'A wizard in the mountains thousands of miles away didn't like to see so many folk being so happy. So, he came during the night and put a padlock and chain round the root of the tree and locked it. If they could only dig that chain up, burst the chain and padlock, the Tree of Happiness would blossom fruit once more. But they'll never know by me!' So, they sat and talked, they talked and cracked, all the wee animals round the foot of the tree, oh, for hours into the morning, when they all bade each other good morning.

'Now before we go,' they said to each other, 'you remember peace and good will among us all for one day, because this is the day the fairies come out, the First of May.' They all bade each other good-bye and away they went. Now True sitting up the tree still cannot see.

He said to himself, 'That's the queerest thing ever I heard in my life. But it could be true . . . I've never heard animals talking before. But there's nothing says it could not be true.' So, down he goes, slides down the tree. He said, 'I wonder if it's true . . . these animals talking – could it be if I did the things that they said, maybe I could be all right, I could see again?'

So, he crept on his hands and knees away through the forest and he kept grabbing with his fingers through the grass. He knew in his own mind it was the First day in May. And he got a buttercup, squeezed it into one eye and the wee taste of dew that was in the buttercup went into his eye. And he opened his eye – he could see with one eye! And he looked round, there were dozens of buttercups and every one full of wee drips of dew. He caught one and squeezed it into his other eye – he could see! He was happy and dancing, lifting all the buttercups and squeezing them in his eyes with excitement. He could see as good as ever!

So, happy and excited he sat down and said, 'I can see again! If that was true about them saying how I could see, then it must be true the rest of the things I heard. It must be! But what am I going to do? This is the First of May and when the sun comes up all the dew will be gone, and the poor king will have to wait a year before he can see. But I know what I'll do . . .' He rumbled in his pockets and got a wee tinder box, a tin box with a wee lid on full of flint and tinder. He emptied it and went to every wee buttercup he could get, poured all the drips of dew into the wee tin box till he had about a tablespoonful off the wee buttercups. And he put the lid back on, kept the box tight in his hand and wrapped his hankie round it to keep the sun from getting near it. Then he set off for the king's palace. He walked and walked on and on and on. He would not halt and would not rest. He kept this box in his hand, walked up to the king's palace, met the guards.

They said, 'Where are you going? What's your name?

He says, 'I'm True.'

They said, 'Are you? What do you want?

He said, 'I want to see the king.'

'What do you want to see the king for?'

He said, 'I've come to cure the king's eyes.'

And when the guards heard this, they cried, 'Someone's come to cure the king's eyes!' The word passed through. Up to the butler, up to the cook, they heard, everybody heard it – 'somebody's come to cure the king's eyes!' And the king was sitting blind on his big throne inside the great big hall, when he hears the voices in the courtyard. And he heard a door opening. In comes the head footman.

'Your Majesty,' he says, 'there's a man at the door saying that he's come to cure your eyes.'

'Never,' says the king, 'no one can cure my eyes. My eyes are gone for good.'

So, True came in and bowed before the king.

He said, 'Your Majesty, my lord, I've come to cure your eyes.'

'If you would only cure my eyes,' he said, 'make me see once again, I'll make you the richest man in the country.'

'I don't want riches, Your Majesty, I only want to help you.' So, he opened the king's eyes and took his wee tin box, teemed a wee drop of the dew in one eye. And the king opened his eye – the king could see! And he teemed a wee drop more dew out of the wee buttercups into the king's other eye – and the king could see! The king was happy and delighted. He threw his arms round True's neck and cuddled him.

'You're a great man,' he said, 'to make me see again! Now where have you come from?'

So True told him, 'My brother poked my eyes out with a fiery stick.'

'Do you want me to go and get your brother? I'll hang him to the highest tree!' the king said.

'No, no,' says True, 'he's my brother and I couldn't do that to him, never. I could never do that to him. But, Your Majesty, I'll have to go.'

'No, no,' says the king, 'you cannot go, you must stay with me! I'll give you riches, I'll give you money, anything you want in this world.'

'Well,' says True, 'I'll stay a wee while.'

So, he stayed a while with the king and the king thought the world of him. The king had a lovely young daughter who fell in love with True. And she and True got married in the castle and the king was proud as could be.

So one day True was sitting and he said to the king, 'You know . . .' He told the king his story.

'Well,' the king said, 'I would like fine if such a thing could happen, for the well – it's in my kingdom! I heard about it, but I don't know if it's true or not about this Well of Health and the Tree of Happiness.

'If it was true,' he said, 'about the cure for your eyes and I got the cure for both our eyesight, it must be true . . .'

'Well,' said the king, 'I'll tell you what to do; you go and see if you can do anything for these things. And I'll look after everything here till you come back.'

So, True gets a horse and away he goes riding on and on and on till he comes to this village and meets all the folk. He asks them about the well.

They tell him, 'Yes, we have the well, but it's no use now. It used to be a great well: it doesn't matter what you suffered from, it would cure you. But within the last few years the water is just like any other water.'

So he said, 'I know what's the cause of it.'

And this head mayor of the town says, 'We'll give you three bags of gold, three donkeys loaded with gold, if you can tell us what's the cause of it, because we love our Well of Health.'

He says, 'Under the stepping stone is a black bullfrog. You take him out and kill him, and try your water then!' Oh, within minutes two men lifted all the flagstones up and sitting in below one stone was a big black frog. This man killed it with a spade!

And who came up but an old crippled man with a lame leg walking, dragging his leg beside him. 'What's going on here, what's going on at the well?' So, they told the old crippled man and the old man got his wee cup, ducked it in the well, filled it full of water. And he drank it. You see, within minutes the old crippled man could have danced a jig! There was nothing to do with him – as healthy as could be – gone was his crippled leg with this beautiful water of the well. So the head mayor of the town took True up and gave him three donkeys loaded with gold.

'Ah, but I do not want them,' says True. 'I'll get them on the road back. I've another job to do before that.'

So on he goes, rides on and on and on till he comes to another village. He asks about the Tree of Happiness.

'Oh yes,' the folk said, 'there's a Tree of Happiness in the green in the middle of the park. But it's no use now, no use, it's only an old withered tree, never any more lovely fruit comes on it; it used to make us all happy.'

'Ah, but,' he said, 'I know what's the cause of it!'

So they sent for the head mayor of the town to tell him that they'd found a man who knew the trouble with the tree. And all the people gathered round. True says, 'Dig down under the roots of that tree! A wizard from a faraway land, a faraway mountain, didn't want to see youse folk being so happy from the fruit from the Tree of Happiness; he came at night and put a chain under the tree and padlocked it. So dig down!'

Two men within minutes got two spades and dug down in below the tree, and round the tree was a big chain with a padlock on it made of brass. They got a big spade, a big pick and hatchet and cut the chain. Folk looked up – the tree was all green and lovely fruit was hanging from it. And this woman came up crying, weeping her heart out. She kept on weeping and weeping.

The mayor of the town says, 'Let's try out our tree! Here, lady, forget about your crying, take a bite of that fruit!'

The lady took a bite of the fruit. You see, within minutes she was dancing, singing and clapping her hands with gladness! No more crying.

'Come,' says the mayor of the town to True, 'there are three donkeys waiting on you loaded with gold.'

'Well,' says True, 'I've proved my point; I did what I set out to do, cured your tree.'

Says the mayor of the town, 'We're happy!' And they gave him the three donkeys loaded with gold. True goes back, gets his other three donkeys loaded with gold from the first village for bringing back their water. And he goes home to his palace, gives three donkeys to the king.

He says, 'I don't need all this gold.' Oh, and he met his young princess and was very happy to see her.

So, he lived in the castle for about a year, when one day he sees this man coming walking up, his clothes all torn, no boots on his feet, nothing, and he's begging from place to place. True looked again; this was his brother Untrue.

He says to the guards, 'Arrest that man and bring him up here before the king!'

So, they arrested Untrue, fetched him up before the king and True. Now True was well in with the king, being his son-in-law, and the king made him as high up in the court as he could.

Untrue was taken up and charged with begging in the streets. 'What has he got to say for himself?'

He said, 'I've nothing to say for myself; I'm a poor man and I must beg.'

'Well,' True said, 'what's your name?'

He said, 'My name is Untrue.'

And he says, 'Why do they call you Untrue? Are you untrue?'

'Yes, I'm untrue. And I'm in misery because once upon a time I had a brother – we called him True. I learned a lesson; my brother and I fought and I poked out his eyes with a blazing stick from the fire, and I've suffered for it ever since.'

'Well,' he says, 'what happened to your brother?'

He said, 'He probably wandered and died in the forest,

eaten by wild beasts because he was blind. And I'm sorry for it ever since.'

So True says to him, 'Take a look at me – who am I?'

And Untrue looked again. He said, 'I can't believe it, I can't believe it . . . you've got eyes! With the argument that was in my heart I poked my brother's eyes out.'

'I'm your brother,' says True, 'I'm your brother! You're Untrue, my brother, so I'm not going to punish you. But I'm going to tell you something; do you know what night this is?'

'No,' says Untrue, 'I don't know what night it is.'

He says, 'This is the last night in April, the same night as you left me one year ago when you poked my eyes out.'

'That's right,' says Untrue.

'Well, when I left you, I went up a tree and all the wee animals gathered round. They told all their secrets and I heard them. I got my eyes cured and I did a lot of other things, got plenty of riches, gold, I'll never need to want the rest of my life from what I heard. You go back to the same tree in the forest, near to where you poked my eyes out, and go up that tree. Listen to the animals – you might learn something to your advantage. And I'm going to let you go,' says True.

So away goes Untrue when he gets free. He travels on and on, and on and on, lands back in the forest at the same tree near to where True had kindled the fire a year before, where he'd poked his brother's eyes out. And he climbs the tree. He sits, sits and sits till midnight, till the last day in April passes away, till it comes the First morning in May. And he's watching – he could see. All the wee animals gathered round. The wolf, the fox, the rabbit, the hare, the hedgehog, the weasel, the stoat, every little animal, even the wee dormouse, gathered round the foot of the tree.

'Well,' says the hare, 'time has come again. Another year has passed away into history and once more this morning is the First of May, the day once again when we all share good will towards each other, and we share our secrets.'

'Aha,' says the fox, 'nah, nah-nah! Did you not hear what happened since we were here last? Somebody else heard our secrets . . . the king has been cured, the Well of Health works again and the Tree of Happiness bears fruit. So, I think from this morning on we'll tell no more secrets!'

And Untrue's sitting up the tree fairly heart-broken! He was that sorry to hear he wasn't going to get any secrets that he slipped off the top of the tree – slipped and fell, broke his neck, landed right in among the wee animals. And all the wee animals ran away for their lives.

Untrue lay under the tree, dead with his broken neck. The wee animals went and spread out, and never met after that to tell any more secrets.

True lived with his wife the princess in the palace with the king. When the king died he got to be king and True was the greatest king of the country!

And that's the last of my wee story.

The Night of Peace

Then God spoke to all the animals and He told them, 'I know that you are the worst sufferers of all – you are persecuted and hunted by man, and slaughtered and killed in your thousands. But I am going to send Someone who will also take care of you.'

The animals spoke back to God and they said, 'How will we know when He comes?'

And God said, 'You'll know when He comes because I will send a star, a shining star low over the land, and,' He says, 'this star will stop when I send to earth the person I want to teach you. Where that star comes to rest – there my Son shall come to earth.'

And the animals were pleased.

So, that night when Jesus was born, the old wolf came out of his den. He was very hungry. He too had heard the Word of God before that time and all day he had lain in his den so lean and hungry – tonight he would go out and hunt. The moon was up and the stars were shining, and one great star came across the sky! The wolf looked and he saw and he felt peaceful, he felt no violence. He didn't want to kill, he didn't want to hunt, he didn't want anything. So he sat and he looked at the star and the star came to rest not far from where the wolf was: the place to this day is known as Bethlehem.

But he hadn't sat very long when the next one who came out of his den was a fox. The fox too was hungry and was intending to go and hunt that night, travel many many miles to look for his fare. But after he came out of his den, and the moon was shining clear and he saw the star (and he too had heard the Word of God when God spoke to all animals), he felt peaceful and content with the world. He had no urge to kill, he had no urge to steal, no urge to do anything, he just wanted to sit and be peaceful.

So he walked up and he sat down beside the wolf. The wolf and the fox were never really enemies – they kept apart from each other but they never really were enemies. So the wolf turned round and said, 'Well, Mister Fox, I see you're on your hunt tonight again.'

'Oh yes,' he said, 'but I feel very funny. I feel hungry, more than hungry – I've been lying in my den in my cave, hiding out all day, but I've got no urge to kill, no urge to steal – and it overpowers my hunger pangs.'

'The same with me,' says the wolf, 'I feel the same way. You remember that God told us that one night He was going to send His Son to earth to walk among animals and people and teach them the way this earth should be run?'

'Aye,' says the fox, 'I got word of that too.'

'Well, I doubt,' says the wolf, 'this is the night.'

So the two of them sat talking for a wee while, when who comes stotting down his path but a big brown hare! And he came to a full stop beside the wolf and the fox. And the wolf paid him no heed and neither did the fox. The hare was amazed. Otherwise he would have stopped, terrified. But he felt no fear! Any other time he'd have been off like a shot in case the wolf or the fox would get him. He sat with his ears straight up!

And it was the wolf who spoke, 'Well, Mister Hare, I see you're off on your rambles tonight again.'

'Well,' the hare said, 'I was off down the valley to the farm. A grass field is there and I was off to fill my belly and have a feed. But I have no inclination tonight . . . I feel hungry but I've no inclination to eat. I feel so peaceful and quiet,' he said, 'I feel at peace with the world. Even you two – I feel at peace with you although you're my enemies.'

'Oh!' said the wolf. 'Pay no heed to us tonight! Tonight is the Night of Peace. Have you not heard,' he said, 'the Word of God?'

'Oh yes,' said the hare, 'I've heard the Word of God, that some day He's going to send His Son, God's Son, to walk among us, among all humans and animals, and teach them the Word of God – how animals should be treated on this earth as well as human beings.'

'Well,' said the wolf, 'I doubt tonight is the night. Look, down the valley there, the moon is shining and you'll see the shepherd sitting out with his sheep, and his dogs are beside him! These dogs have picked up our scent long long ago, the scent of the wolf and the fox and probably the scent of you too. And they pay no heed, they too are peaceful. So is the shepherd. Tonight I think all animals will be peaceful.'

'Well,' the hare says, 'tonight if you're going to be like that and the fox is going to be like that, why don't we all gather together – you go that way and I'll go this way, and let the fox go another direction! Tell every animal that you meet on your way that tonight is the night God has sent His Son to earth, and we shall have a night of peace – no animal shall destroy another.'

'Well,' says the wolf, 'that would be a very good plan, for tonight I feel very funny – I feel so happy although I'm hungry!'

So the wolf went in one direction, the fox went in another direction and the hare went another. The hare met all the small mammals along the way and he told them the same thing – from the very little shrew-mouse to the hedgehog, the rat, the vole and the water vole – and everyone felt the same.

So the fox went off and he met many other animals – he met the rabbits and he met the badger, he met the stoat and he met the weasel – he met them all and told them the same thing: 'This is the Night of Peace.'

So the wolf went off and he wandered in the same way. He met the deer – the deer was amazed because the wolf never chased him – and the deer was peaceful. The wolf travelled on and on and he walked among the cattle. The cattle were peaceful. Till he came to the donkey – the donkey was peacefully grazing. And the wolf walked up.

He says to the donkey, 'Hello!'

'Oh!' says the donkey. 'I see you're on your travels tonight once again,' and the donkey stood still.

He said to the donkey, 'Tonight all the animals are at peace.'

'That's true,' said the donkey, 'all the animals are at peace! Why have you come to disturb me?'

'I have not come to disturb you,' he said. 'I have come to tell you the good news.'

The donkey says, 'Look, Mister Wolf, you don't have to come tell me the news. I too, more than anyone else, have heard the Voice of God! And this night,' he said, 'is the night that God's Son is born. Let us all be at peace!'

And that night, the whole night through, all the animals on the hills, the mountains, in valleys and woods were at peace with each other. No one touched another, no one killed another, and for the whole night out they celebrated the coming of Jesus Christ to earth!

That story was told to me . . . well, when my brother George got a terrible cut on his leg – he would have been five and I would have been three. He had crawled upon the sharp lid of a pot, he had cut his knee on it. And my father said (it must have been about Christmas time), 'Come and I'll tell you a wee holy story that's been taught to me by my father,' to keep him from crying, you know! And he said, 'God help us, it's not too bad, your leg – it's nothing to worry about!' see, trying to calm the child. And he told us the story about the animals having peace and quietness among themselves for one night during the coming of Jesus Christ to the earth. Probably the young child didn't understand much about the story – but he listened and probably the way that my father told it to him soothed him, kept him quiet, made him forget about this cut that he had got on his knee.

The Tramp and the Bull

It was a cold winter's morning when the old tramp awoke. He had slept under a tree all night and it was the cold that wakened him. The tramp had little breakfast so he just wrapped his ragged coat around him and thought he would move on the road once more, see if he could find something along the roadway. Now he was one of these old tramps who travelled all over Scotland, wandered the roads, begged a little, got a little from people as he went on his way. He'd lost all sense of time, knew it was winter and that was all. Having travelled far the day before he'd promised himself that the next place or the next village he would come to he would try and get something to eat. But he was in the West Coast of Scotland, well up in the Highlands, and after travelling all day he had not had a bite of meat of any description. Hungry and tired he went on his way, and the days being short it began to get dark once more.

He thought to himself, 'I'll have to find some place to sleep the night even though I have nothing to eat. I must find shelter.' Because it was a cold, cold day and he knew it was going to be a cold, cold night. He came along this track in the Western Highlands where farms and houses are few and far between. But some local farmers keep outbuildings on the moors and hills for to feed their cattle during the storms. These buildings have no front, only a back and two sides, no doors of any kind. And this particular one was in a field, surrounded by a large fence. So the tramp thought to himself, 'This'll do for shelter. I'll probably not find another place this night.' By this time it was dark.

So he climbed over the fence, which was a high one, walked into the old shed, gathered all the scattered pieces of dry hay he could find and made himself a little bed in one corner away from the wind; wrapped himself in his ragged coat and lay down hungry and tired. But at least he had found shelter for the night. He had lain for a couple of hours and kind of dovered off, but being so hungry he could hardly sleep. The moon began to come up. It was a frosty night and the stars were shining.

How long the tramp lay he didn't know for sure . . . when lo and behold, the next thing he heard was the sound of a bull, the low 'moah-oa-oa, moa-oahoah, moaoah' of a bull bellowing in the corner of the field!

The tramp said to himself, 'If I'm not wrong, that is a bull! And by the way he's bellowing I think he's wicked!'

Now there was a piece of wood nailed to the fence saying BEWARE OF THE BULL but in the dark the tramp had never seen this. And the poor old soul had climbed the fence. So he lay there and knew the bull was coming closer by its bellowing.

At last he sat up, pulled his ragged coat around him and said, 'Almighty God, You must have called for me this night!' He knew he had no way to reach the fence, maybe a hundred and fifty yards away. And he heard the bull coming closer. He looked up: the moon was shining clear. And a large star was coming across the heavens . . . the old tramp looked up, saw the star shining in the sky, wondered why the star was so bright.

Then lo and behold, the bull came up to the door bellowing and throwing earth over its shoulder. The tramp knew it was wild and he had no chance of escape – when the next thing he saw was a shadow crossing the doorway of the shed where he lay. And he looked – a donkey. It came within five or six yards of him, and the donkey went down on its knees. And the tramp looked: the bull stopped bellowing and the bull came along, a little bit from the donkey, and the bull went down on *his* knees!

The tramp looked up: he saw the moon and he saw the stars, said, 'My God, it must be Christmas Eve!' and the tramp got up, wrapped his ragged coat around him and walked between the bull and the donkey. The bull paid no attention to him, neither did the donkey. And the tramp walked to the fence, climbed over it and walked onto the road.

He looked back, shook his head, and said, 'Thank you, my Lord.'

For he knew in his own mind it was Christmas Eve – for that is when all animals go down on their knees for one hour. And while the animal went down on its knees in that one hour the tramp would be safe – why he felt no fear of the bull when he walked past it.

And that old tramp told this story to my father and me and the children many, many years ago around our camp fireside in Argyll.

That is a true Christmas tale.

Mary and the Seal

Many years ago in a little isle off the West Coast of Scotland – it could be Mull, Tiree, or any island – there lived an old fisherman and his wife. And the old fisherman spent his entire life fishing in the sea and selling whatever fish he couldn't use himself to keep him and his wife and his little daughter alive. They lived in this little cottage by the sea and not far from where they stayed was the village, a very small village – a post office, a hall and some cottages. But everyone knew everyone else. And his cousin also had a house in the village.

This old man and woman had a daughter called Mary and they loved her dearly, she was such a nice child. She helped her father with the fishing and when she was finished helping her father, she always came and helped her mother to do housework and everything else. The father used to set his nets every day in the sea and he used to rise early every morning. Mary used to get up and help her father lift his nets and collect the fish. After that was done she used to help her mother, then went off to school. Everybody was happy for Mary. And her father and mother were so proud of her because she was such a good worker. But she was such a quiet and tender little girl and didn't pay attention to anyone . . . she did her schoolwork in school. But the years passed by and Mary grew till she became a young teenager.

This is where the story really begins, when Mary was about sixteen or seventeen. She always used to borrow her father's boat, every evening in the summertime, and go for a sail to a little island that lay about half a mile from where they stayed, a small island out in the middle of the sea-loch. And Mary used to go out and spend all her spare time on the island. Every time she'd finished her day's work with her father and helped her mother and had her supper, she would say, 'Father, can I borrow your boat?' Even in the wintertime sometimes, when the sea wasn't too rough, she would go out there and spend her time. Her father and mother never paid any attention because Mary's spare time was her own time; when her work was finished she could do what she liked. Till one day.

Her mother used to walk down to the small village to the post office where they bought their small quantity of messages and did their shopping; it was the only place they could buy any supplies.

She heard two old women nattering to each other. Mary's mother's back was turned at the time but she overheard the two old women. They were busy talking about Mary.

'Och,' one woman said, 'she's such a nice girl, but she's so quiet. She doesn't come to any of the dances and she doesn't even have a boyfriend. She doesn't do anything – we have our ceilidhs and we have our things and we never see her come, she never even pays us a visit. Such a nice quiet girl, all she wants to do, she tells me, is to take her boat and she rows over to the island and spends all her time there on the island. Never even comes and has a wee timey* – when our children have their shows and activities in school she never puts in an appearance! And her mother and father are such decent people . . . even her Uncle Lachy gets upset!'

* has a wee timey – spends a while with someone

This was the first time her mother had heard these whispers, so she paid little attention. She came home, and she was a wee bit upset. And the next time she went back to the village she heard the same whispers again – this began to get into her mind, she began to think. But otherwise Mary was just a natural girl: she helped her daddy and she asked her mummy if there was anything she could do, helped her to do everything in the house, and she was natural in every way. But she kept herself to herself.

One evening it was suppertime once more, and after supper Mary said, 'Daddy, can I borrow your boat?'

'Oh yes, Mary, my dear,' he said, 'you can borrow the boat. I'm sure I'm finished – we've finished our day's work. You can have the boat.'

It wasn't far to row the little boat, maybe several hundred yards to the wee island in the loch. And the old woman and the old man sat by the fire.

Once Mary had walked out the door and said good-bye to her father and mother, the old woman turned round and said to her husband, 'There she goes again. That's her gone again.'

Mary's father turned round and he said, 'What do you mean? Margaret, what do you mean – you know Mary always goes off, an-and-and enjoys herself in the boat.'

'Angus, you don't know what I mean: it's not you that has got to go down to the village and listen to the whispers of the people, and the talk and the wagging tongues.'

He says, 'Woman, what are you talking about?'

She says, 'I'm talking about your daughter.'

Angus didn't know what to say. He said, 'What's wrong with my daughter? I'm sure she works hard and she deserves a little time by herself – what's the trouble, was there something that you needed done that she didn't do?'

'Not at all,' she said, 'that's not what I'm talking about.'

'Well, tell me what you're trying to say!'

'Angus, it's Mary – the people in the village are beginning to talk.'

'And what are they saying about my daughter?' And he started to get angry.

'They're talking about Mary going off herself in her boat to the island and spending all her time there; she's done that now for close on five years. And they say she doesn't go to any dances, she doesn't go to any parties and she doesn't accept any invitations to go anywhere and she has no boyfriend! And the wagging tongues in the village are talking about this. It's getting through to me and I just don't like it.'

'Well,' he said, 'Mother, I'm sure there's nothing in the world that should upset you about that; I'm sure Mary's minding her own business! And if she's out there, she's no skylarking with some young man – would you rather have her skylarking around the village with some young man or something? And destroying herself and bringing back a baby or something to you – would you enjoy that better?'

'It's not that, Angus, it's just that Mary is so unsociable.'

But anyway, they argued and bargued* for about an hour and they couldn't get any further. By the time they were finished Mary came in again. She was so radiant and happy.

She came over, kissed her mother and kissed her daddy, said, 'Daddy, I pulled the boat up on the beach, and everything's all right.'

He says, 'All right, Daughter, that's nice.'

'And, Daddy, the tide is coming in and some of the corks of the net are nearly sunk, so I think we'll have a good

---

* argued and bargued – quarreled

fishing in the morning. I'll be up bright and early to give you a hand.'

He said, 'Thank you, Mary, very much.'

And she kissed her mother and said, 'I'll just have a small something to eat and I'll go to bed.'

But anyway, the old woman was unsettled. 'There she goes again,' she says, 'that's all we get.'

'Well,' he says, 'what more do you expect? She's doing her best, Mother. She's enjoying herself.'

'What is she doing on that island? That's what I want to know.'

Said the old man to Margaret, 'Well, she's no doing any harm out there.'

So the next morning they were up bright and early, had their breakfast. And Mary went out with her father, collected the nets, collected the fish, and they graded the fish and kept some for themselves. Then they went into the village and sold the rest, came back home, had their supper. It was a beautiful day.

And Mary said, 'Is there anything you want me to do, Mother?'

'Well no, Mary, everything is properly done: the washing's finished and the cleaning's finished, and I was just making some jam; and I'm sure your father's going to sit down and have a rest because he's had a hard day.'

Mary turned round and she said, 'Father, could I borrow your boat?' once again.

'I'm sure, my dear,' he says, 'you can have the boat. Take the boat. Now be careful because there might be a rise of a storm.'

'I'll be all right, Father,' she said, 'I don't think it's going to – the sky looks so quiet and peaceful. I doubt if we'll have a storm the night.' And away she goes.

But as soon as she takes off in the boat, oh, her mother gets up. 'That's it, there she goes again! To put my mind at rest, would you do something for me?'

Angus says, 'What is it you want now, woman?'

'Look,' she said, 'would you relieve my mind for me: would you go down and borrow Lachy's boat, your cousin Lachy's boat, and row out to the island and see what Mary does when she goes there? It'll put my mind at rest.'

'That's no reason for me to go out,' he said. 'Let the lassie enjoy herself if she wants to enjoy herself! There's no reason for me to go out – I'm sure there's no-one within miles. Maybe she's wading on the beach and she sits there, an-and-and maybe she has some books with her, and she – she likes to be by herself.'

But no. She says, 'Look, do something for me, husband! Would you go out, Angus, and see what she does?'

So Angus said, 'Och, dash it, woman! To keep you happy, I'll go out and see what she's doing. It's only a waste of time anyway.'

So he walks down; it was only about two hundred yards down to Lachy's cottage. Lachy had the same kind of boat. He was sitting at the fire; he had never married; their fathers had been brothers. Lachy stayed in this cottage, he was an old retired seaman and he always liked to keep a boat.

'Well, it's yourself, Angus!' he said, 'Come away in. And come you, sit down and we'll have a wee dram.'

'No,' he said, 'Angus, I'm not here for a dram.'

'Well, what sent you down? It's not often you come for a visit.'

'I was wondering,' he said, 'if you would let me borrow your boat for a few minutes?'

And Lachy said, 'Well, what's the trouble?'

'Ach, it's no trouble, really, I was just wanting to borrow your boat for maybe half an hour or so.'

'Well, what is wrong with your own boat?'

'Och, Mary's using it.'

And Lachy said, 'Och, that's Mary off on her gallivant to the island again. And you want to follow the lassie and see what she's doing. If I was you I would leave her alone. Come on, sit down and have a dram with me and forget about it.'

But old Angus was so persistent. 'I want to borrow your boat.'

'Well,' he said, 'take the dashit thing and away you go!'

He takes the boat and he rows across to the island and he lands on the small beach. There was Mary's boat beached. And he pulls his cousin Lachy's boat up beside Mary's, and beaches it. And he walks up a path – it was well worn because Mary had walked up this path many many times – he follows the path up, goes over a little knowe. There are some rocks and a few trees, and down at the back of the island is a small kind of valley-shaped place that leads out to the sea. Then there's a beach, and on the beach is a large rock. And beside the rock is a wee green patch.

Old Angus came walking up, taking his time, looked all around and looked all around. There were a few seagulls flying around and a few birds wading along the beach because the tide was on the ebb. And he heard the laughing coming on, giggling and laughing – this was Mary – carrying on. And he came up over the knowe, he looked down; here was Mary with a large seal, a grey seal. And they were having the greatest fun you've ever seen: they were wrestling in the sand, carrying on and laughing, the seal was grunting and Mary was flinging her arms around the seal!

So Angus stopped, he sat down and watched for a wee while. He said, 'Ach, I'm sure she's doing no harm, it's only a seal. And her mother was so worried about it. She's enjoying herself; probably she's reared it up from a pup and she comes over to feed it, and I'm sure it won't do her any harm. She's better playing with a seal than carrying on with a young bachal as far as I'm concerned!'

So, he takes his boat and he rows home, gives his cousin Lachy back the boat, lights his pipe and walks up to his own home. He comes in through the door and his old wife, old Margaret, is waiting on him.

She said, 'You're home, Angus.'

'Aye, I'm home, Margaret, I'm home. And thanks be praised to God I am home!'

'Did you see Mary?'

'Of course I saw Mary. She's out on the island.'

'And what is she doing? Is she sitting – what is she doing?' He said, 'She's enjoying herself.'

Old Margaret said, 'What way is she enjoying herself – is she wading on the beach or something?'

'No, she's not wading on the beach.'

'Is she reading?'

'No she's not reading.' He said, 'She's playing herself with a seal.'

'What did you say?'

'She's playing herself – she has the best company in the world and she's enjoying herself – she's playing with a seal! A large grey seal. They're having great fun and I didn't interfere.'

She said, 'Angus, Mary's enchanted. It's one of the sea-people that's taken over. Your daughter is finished – ruined for evermore. I've heard stories from my grandmother how the sea-people take over a person and take them away for evermore, they're never seen again – she's enchanted. What kind of a seal was it?'

'It was a grey seal and they were having good fun so I didn't interfere.'

She said, 'If you want to protect your daughter and you want to have your daughter for any length of time, you'd better get rid of the seal.'

He says, 'Margaret, I couldn't interfere with them. It's Mary's pet.'

'I don't care if it's Mary's pet or no,' she said. 'Tomorrow morning you will take your gun and go out, and instead of going to the fish you'll go out and you'll shoot that seal and destroy it for evermore!'

'But it's Mary's pet,' he said. 'She probably reared it up unknown to us, she probably reared it up from a young pup, and it's not for me to destroy the seal, the thing she has to play with.'

'I'm sure she can find plenty of company in the village instead of going out there to the island!'

But the argument went on, and they argued and argued and finally old Margaret won. He lighted his pipe to have a smoke before going to bed.

'Well,' he said, 'in the morning I'll go out and see.'

Then Mary came home and she was so radiant and so bright, so happy. She came in and kissed her daddy and kissed her mummy. She had a cup of tea and asked Mummy and Daddy if they needed anything or wanted anything done.

And they said, 'No, Mary.'

The old woman was a wee bit kind of dubious. She wasn't just a wee bit too pleased. And Mary saw this.

She said, 'Is there something wrong, Mother?'

'No, Mary,' she said, 'there's nothing wrong.'

'Well, I'm going off to my bed.' Mary went to her bed. In these cottages in times long ago in the little crofts, the elderly people stayed down on the floor and there was a small ladder that led up to the garret in the roof. If you had any children they had their beds in the garret. Mary lived upstairs.

So the next morning Angus got up early. And before he even had any breakfast, he went to the back of the house and took his gun. He loaded his gun and took his boat and he rowed out to the island, before Mary was up. And he walked up the path, the way Mary usually went, over the little hillock, down the little path to the little green part beside the bare rock – sure enough, sitting there sunning himself in the morning sun was the seal.

Angus crept up as close as he could – he fired the shot at the seal, hit the seal. And the seal just reared up – fell, and then crawled, made its way into the sea, hobbled its way into the water and disappeared. 'That's got you,' he said.

And then he felt queer. A funny sensation came over him. And he sat down, he felt so funny – as if he had shot his wife or his daughter. A sadness came over him. And he sat for a long while, then he left the gun down beside him and he looked at the gun . . . he felt that he had done something terrible. He felt so queer.

So he picked up the gun, walked back to his boat and he could barely walk, he felt so sick. He put the gun in the boat. He sat for a while before he could even take off in the boat and he had the queer sensation, a feeling of loss was within him, a terrible feeling of loss – that something he had done could never be undone . . . he could hardly row the boat. But he finally made his way back to the mainland, tied up his boat, picked up the gun, and put it back in the cupboard. He walked in and old Margaret was sitting there.

'You're back, Angus.'

'Yes I'm back.'

She said, 'Did you do what I told you to do?'

'Yes, Mother,' he said, 'I did what you – what you told me to do.'

'Did you see the seal?'

'Yes, I saw the seal. And I shot the seal.'

She sat down. 'Are you wanting . . .'

'No, I don't want any breakfast,' he said.

She says, 'Are you feeling . . .'

'No, I'm not feeling very well. I'm not feeling very well at all.'

'What's wrong with you?'

'Well,' he says, 'I feel terrible, I feel queer and I feel so kind of sad . . . I've done something wrong and you forced me to it, I hope in the future that you'll be sorry for it.'

'Och,' she said, 'it's only a seal!'

But they said no more. By this time Mary had come down.

She said, 'Good morning, Father; good morning, Mother,' and she sat down at the table as radiant as a flower and had some breakfast. 'Are you not eating, Daddy?'

'No,' he said, 'Daughter, I don't . . .'

'Are you not feeling very well?' And she came over and stroked her father's head. 'Are you not feeling very well, Father?'

'Oh, I'm feeling fine, Mary. I'm just not, just – what I should be.' And the mother tried to hide her face in case Mary could see something in her face that would – a giveaway in her face, you know.

'Well,' she says, 'Father, are you ready to go out to lift the net?'

'Well, Mary, to tell you the truth, I don't think the tide'll be on the – the out-going tide won't be for a while yet. No, I think I'll sit here and have a smoke.'

'Mother,' she says, 'are you needing anything done?'

'No, Mary, we don't need anything done.'

Now they wanted to try and be as canny with her as possible. They didn't want to upset her in any way.

And the mother said, 'No, Mary, I think everything's done. There's only a little cleaning to be done and I think I'll manage.'

Mary says, 'Well, after I milk the cow, Father, would it be all right if I take the boat?'

'Och, yes, Daughter, go ahead and help yourself to the boat,' he said, 'I'm sure you can have the boat any time. You don't need to ask me for the boat, just take it whenever you feel like it.'

So Mary milked the cow, brought in the milk and set the basins for the cream, and did everything that was needing to be done. She said, 'Goodbye, Mother, I'll see you in a while. I'm just going off for a while to be by myself – I'll be back before very long.'

Mother said, 'There she goes again! If you tell me it's true, she'll be home sadder and wiser.'

But old Angus never said a word. He just sat and smoked his pipe. And he still had this – as if a lump were in his heart. And he was under deep depression, just didn't want to get up, just wanted to sit. He had this great terrible feeling of loss.

So Mary rowed the boat over to the island. And he sat by the fire and he smoked and he smoked and he smoked. Maggie called him for dinner and the day passed by, but Mary never returned. Evening meal came, and Mary never returned. Her mother began to get worried.

She came down and she said, 'Angus, has Mary come home? It'll soon be time for milking the cow again.'

'No,' he said, 'Mary has never come.'

'Perhaps,' she said, 'she – would you go down and see if the boat's in? Has she tied up the boat? Maybe she walked

down to the village.' Angus went out and there was no sign
of the boat.

'No,' he said, 'the boat—'

'Well, she's not home. If the boat's not home, she's not
home,' she said. 'I doubt something's happened to her . . .
I doubt something's happened to her – Angus, you'll have
to go and see what, you'll have to go out to the island. Go
down and get Lachy's boat and go out to the island and see.'

So Angus goes down, just walks down and takes Lachy's
boat, never asks permission, just pulls the rope, unties the
rope and jumps in the boat. He doesn't – he had the feeling
that he doesn't even worry what happens, he's so upset. And
he rows out to the island and there's Mary's boat. And he
pulls the boat in because the beach was quite shallow. And
he lays the boat beside Mary's boat, his own boat. And he
walks up the path, over the little hillock, down by the big
rock to the little bay and the green patch beside the big rock,
and walks right down where he saw the seal. He looks. The
side of the rock was splattered with the blood where he had
shot the seal. And he walks round the whole island, which
wasn't very big, walks the whole island round – all he saw
was a few spots of blood. Nowhere did he find Mary. Mary
had completely disappeared, there wasn't a sign of her, not
even a footprint. And he walked round once, he walked
round twice and he went round a third time; every tree,
every bush, every rock he searched, but Mary was gone.

And he felt so sad. 'What could happen to Mary, my poor
wee Mary, what happened to her?'

Then at the very last he came back once again to the rock
where he had shot the seal – and he looked out to sea, the
tide was on the ebb. And he stood, looked for a long long
while. And he looked at the rock, saw the blood was drying
in the sun. And he looked again, then – all in a moment

up come two seals, two grey seals, and they come right out of the water, barely more than twenty-five yards from where he stood! And they look at him. They look directly at him – then disappear back down in the water. And he had this queer feeling that he was never going to see Mary anymore.

So he took his boat and he rowed home, tied up his boat. Just the one boat, took his own boat, left Lachy's boat on the island.

He sat down beside the fire. His wife Margaret came to him.

She said, 'Did you see Mary?'

'No,' he said, 'I never saw Mary. I never saw Mary, I searched the entire island for Mary and Mary is gone. And look, between you and me, she's gone for ever. We'll never see Mary again.'

And they waited and they waited, and they waited for the entire days of their lives, but Mary never returned.

And that is the end of my tale.

That was a Gaelic tale from the Western Isles. That story was told to me when I was only about fifteen years of age, doing the stone-dyking in Argyll at Auchindrain with a mason, Mr Neil McCallum. He was from crofting stock; he was a crofter, his brother was a crofter. And just to sit there listening . . . I can still hear his voice in my ears; you know, his voice is still there after, maybe, nearly forty years. And every little detail is imprinted in my memory. And when I tell you the story, I try to get as close as possible to the way that he spoke to me. Do you understand what I mean?

The Boy, the Toad and the Snake

Many many years ago there once lived a shepherd and his wife who had a cottage by the roadside. The shepherd was a busy man and looked after his sheep, and he was a very good husband. They had one little boy. Both of them loved this boy dearly.

And one night the father says to the boy, 'Son, you're coming up for the age now, I think it's about time that we should send you to school.' In these days you went to school in your bare feet. You wore no boots.

And because the boy had never been to the school before he said, 'Daddy, how do I get to school?'

'Well,' he said, 'your mother will take you the first day. And then the second or the third day you go to school, you go by yourself. Learn to read and write and get all your education. It's only about a mile along the road.'

'Okay,' says the boy. 'Daddy, I would like that very much. I could play with the rest of the boys.'

'Now,' the father says, 'whatever you do on your way back and forward to school, if you meet any animals on the road, any squirrels or rats or anything – don't interfere with them – they're nature's children, don't interfere.'

'Okay,' says the boy.

So the first day the mother took him to school, introduced him to the teacher. And she went away back home. The boy really enjoyed himself. Oh, he had a good day in the school! He really loved it.

But it was the month of May, summertime. As usual, he wore no boots on his feet. And one morning he said good-bye to his mummy and set off to school.

He had not travelled very far along the road when he came upon, in the middle of the road in his path, a toad and a snake. And the snake was trying to swallow the toad. The toad was trying his best to master the snake. It was a toad, a black toad. The two of them were doing battle in the middle of the road.

The boy stopped, he took a stick; and he liked snakes so he killed the toad. And the snake went away through the grass. He had battered the toad till he'd killed it.

'There,' he said, 'that'll learn you not to fight a wee snake. I like wee snakes. You, you ugly toad, I've killed you!'

He left it lying in the road.

So the summer wore on and the sun beat down. The horses passing by in these days tramped on the toad and they broke it all up. The toad disintegrated on the road. The end of summer passed. The school term began again.

One day the boy was in a hurry coming home from school running hard, and he stepped on the toad – jag! into his heel. He never thought anything of it. The boy came home, had his supper. The next day he wakened up.

His mummy said, 'Are you going to school?'

'No, Mummy,' he said, 'I can't go to school. My foot . . . my heel is terribly sore. I've got a terrible sore heel.'

She said, 'Well, you had better stay off school if you've got a sore heel.' So, by the night-time his father had come back it was worse. His heel was swelled up and inflamed.

He said, 'I doubt we'll have to get the quacks up to see your heel.' Quacks they were called in these days; there were no doctors. They sent for the quack and he came. He looked at the boy's heel.

He said, 'Och, it's just, maybe a thorn, a prick by a thorn. Just put a poultice on it. It will be okay.'

They put an oatmeal poultice on it. But no. Before the night was out the boy's leg was swelled right out. The boy got sick and pale and wan. His memory began to go. But his leg never got any better. It remained swollen and sore. They tried every medicine under the sun. It was no use.

Two weeks passed by. And the boy's leg was no better. He could not walk. So the mother and father were terribly upset, very, very upset. And the boy could not walk at all. So, it came a beautiful day.

The father says to the mother, 'Look, that laddie hasn't got very much fresh air in this house. Tomorrow you might take him outside, take him out to the garden. Let him sit for a wee while and rest his foot, because it's not getting any better day out and day in. I don't know what's wrong with it. I've had all the quacks up and everybody under the sun has seen it, but it's not getting any better.'

So the woman took the wee laddie out in the garden. She left him and the wee laddie lay down with his bare foot, his two bare feet stretched out. His sore heel was swelled right out. He wasn't sick, but his leg wasn't getting any better.

When lo and behold he's sitting with his foot stretched out on the grass, the first thing he sees coming along the grass is a snake.

The snake came up, head going, tail going out and in, all around, in all directions, tongue going out and in, the forked tongue and circling round about. It came up close, right to the boy's heel, to the sore part of the heel and it started – it sucked, suck, suck, suck, suck, sucked – on the heel. When the snake started to suck, the pain went away. The boy fell sound asleep.

By this time who came back but the father, into the house.
He says, 'Where's the laddie?'

She said, 'He's out in the garden.'

He said, 'Did you leave him out there all day?'

She says, 'Aye, I left him out. I've never heard a word
from him.'

He said, 'Maybe he's dead, maybe his leg killed him!'

And the shepherd runs out. He looks. There's a big
adder about three feet long sucking the boy's heel! And
the swelling was nearly away from the boy's leg. Once the
man's shadow comes within reach of the adder the adder
disappears among the grass. And the man looks down.

He runs into the house and tells his wife, 'Come out quick,
your wean has been bit by a snake! He's going to die!'

The woman comes and she lifts her laddie's leg up. The
wee laddie is still sound asleep.

'His leg's better,' she said. 'The swelling is gone!'

The man lifted his heel up.

'But,' he said, 'I saw a snake sucking his heel. It was biting
him!'

She says, 'Wait a minute!'

The woman bends down, picks up the laddie's foot. All
the redness is gone from his heel and the wound is open.
The man looks at the wound, and sticking out of it is a bone,
very small. The man reaches down and pulls the bone out;
it was a piece of bone about an inch long in the boy's heel.

By this time the wee boy wakens up. He gets up and onto
his feet. He runs about!

'Oh,' he says, 'Mummy, Mummy, I had a dream, a great
dream that a snake came and sucked my leg and made my foot
better! I'm all right now. There's no pain, nothing in my leg.'

The man said, 'Son, look, *that's* what I took out of your
foot! There was a snake sucking your foot.'

'Oh, Daddy,' he said, 'I should have told you. Maybe it was my pal, the snake.'

'What pal?' says the man.

'Well,' he said, 'when I started school in the summertime I came across the snake and a toad. They were fighting in the road. And I took a stick, I killed the toad. And the snake went away.'

'Well look,' the man said, '*that* is a piece of the toad's bone that was in your foot and caused you all the trouble. You may be thankful that the snake came back and paid his debt to you, and made your foot better. Nobody in the world could have cured it but the snake. I warned you before: never, never touch any animals you see along the road!'

And from that day on till the laddie was seventy years of age, never again did he ever interfere with a toad or a snake or a wee animal along the way.

Death and the Woodcutter

A long time ago away up in the north of Scotland there lived an old woodcutter in a little cottage in the middle of a great forest. It was an oak forest. He had come there as a young man, brought his young wife with him to take up the little cottage and become a forester, and to take care of the forest. And with his wife he was very happy.

He'd been there for many, many years and understood life and death perfectly well; he'd lost his parents, he'd lost his grandfather and his grandmother just before he and his young wife moved into the forest.

They were not long there before the love of their life came along, a baby, a little girl. And she was called after her mother, Mary. She was the love of the woodcutter's life – he used to sit and tell his little girl stories, of what happened in the forest – if he came across a little deer tangled in the forest, how it was caught in brambles and died because it could not get free. He would tell her of the birds he found, of pigeons, of owls and she would say, 'Daddy, why has these little creatures got to die?' And he'd explain to her. And when she grew up, was able to walk, he would take her with him some days to the forest and point out to her, show her all these things. Yes, he understood death perfectly well.

When she was ten years old there came a very heavy sadness in his life; his wife, Mary's mother, took very sick and after a short illness died. The woodcutter's heart was broke with sorrow but he understood. He explained, 'There was a reason for death, a reason.' Even through his sadness he tried to comfort his little daughter and tell her.

She stayed with her daddy, went to school in the local village nearby. In the weekends he would take her with him to the forest, tell her those stories about life in the forest where he worked.

And naturally she grew up, stayed with her daddy until she became a marriageable age. And because she frequently made visits to the local village she fell in love with the son of the local grocer; Mary got married to him. But she always remembered her mother and the words her daddy had told her. She was very happy and she and her husband visited her daddy many times. Till one day they told him the great news they were going to have a baby of their own!

And the old woodcutter was delighted. He had survived and hoped he would survive a little longer, that he would become a granddad! And so he did – sure enough, a little baby girl was born and was called after her mother, Mary. Granddad still worked alone in the forest in his little cottage. He would make frequent visits to the village and sit there, take the baby on his knee, his little granddaughter. And when she came to listenable age he would tell her stories. She grew up with the love and respect for her old granddad, and she attended the little village school as her mother had done. But when she came about ten, the love of her life was to visit her granddad in his little cottage nearby in the forest.

Now old Granddad loved these visits from his little granddaughter. And he would go to the highest part of the forest where he could see his little house. He'd watch till he saw the smoke coming from the chimney – he knew his little granddaughter would be there – the fire would be kindled, the old iron kettle would be boiling on the hob, the table would be cleaned up, the cups washed, his plates put by and his floor swept, for little Mary had enjoyed doing this for her granddad. She always looked forward to this. She had a little pinny hanging behind the door she put around her waist waiting for Granddad to come in; she knew how to kindle a fire, how to boil a kettle; she was ten years old.

But this morning she said, 'Mummy, it's Saturday and time to visit Granddad.'

'Yes, my dear,' she says.

'Mummy, do we have something for Granddad this morning?'

'Of course, darling, we always have something for Granddad!' She brought out a basket she usually carried with her – a bit of cheese, some homemade scones, some eggs, some butter. 'You take this to Granddad, darling, and tell him we'll come along and see him some other time.'

'Yes, Mummy,' she said and kissed her.

Off she went tripping to Granddad's, quite safe. It wasn't far to go, a little path led to the cottage in the wood, no one would harm her in these days. She came to her granddad's cottage. The door was always open. She placed the little basket on the table and looked around, 'Oh, Granddad, Granddad!' she says. 'This place is a terrible, awfae mess, why don't you clean up?'

But Granddad had foreseen this. He would take his pipe and tap the dottles on the mantelpiece; he would leave his cup and plate on the table, but he would always make sure there were kindling and coal by the fireside and peats for her. And she would come in, 'Oh, Granddad, Granddad, this place is so terrible!' But she would smile to herself, take her little pinafore from behind the door, put it round her waist, a real lady! and begin cleaning up.

But this particular morning as she placed the basket on the table before she even put her little pinafore on, there was a knock at the door, 'knock-knock-knock-knock'.

'I wonder who that could be,' she said to herself, 'Granddad never knocks.' And she went to the door.

There standing was a tall stranger dressed in black from head to toe and she could see that his eyes were pale and glassy, his face was pale and his long fingers were by his side. She had never seen a stranger like this; he was not one of the people from the village.

Not afraid she says, 'Can I help you, sir?'

'Yes,' he said, 'my dear, you can. Is your granddad at home?'

'N-n-no, no, sir, Granddad has not come back from the forest yet; he'll be back in a little while.'

He said, 'Eh, well, I cannot wait, my dear.'

'Well,' she said, 'c-can you, can you leave your name and I'll tell him you called?'

'I'll leave my name,' he said, 'and tell him I'll be coming back a little later.'

'Then who shall I say called? You're not from the village.'

'No, my dear, I'm not from the village,' he said.

'Well, I'll tell him – who called?'

He says, 'Just tell him Death has called, and I'll be coming back a little later.' And he was gone.

Little Mary stood there. She knew all about death, all the stories Granddad had told her; she knew that when death came to take people away you never see them again.

And Granddad waited, he watched from the highest part of the forest the little house but no smoke appeared from the chimney, something was wrong! He looked at his old pocket watch, something was wrong. He made his way to the little cottage and walked in, and there he found her sitting crying, the tears running down her cheeks, the basket on the table. She had never done anything to the house, the fire was black out. And when she saw her granddad she ran and threw her arms round him.

'Granddad, Granddad, please, Granddad, please, quick, Granddad, let's run away!'

'Let's run away, my dear?' says Granddad.

'Yes, Granddad, please, let's run away!'

'Come, come, calm yourself, my child, what is wrong with you?'

'Granddad, the stranger! He came, Granddad, just before you returned and he's coming back, Granddad, to take you away.'

'Take me away, my dear?'

'Yes, Granddad, he's taking you away and I'll never see you again. I'll never have any more stories, Granddad. I'll never be able to come and tidy up for you again. Please, Granddad, please, Granddad, let's run away where he'll never find us!'

'Calm yourself, my child, tell me what is wrong!'

'He came, Granddad, the stranger.'

'The stranger, my dear?'

'Yes, Granddad!'

'D-di-did he give his name to you? D-did-did he tell you who he was, what he wanted?'

'Yes, Granddad, he told me, he said he was Death, Granddad! Death is coming for you! Death is coming to take you away, Granddad, and I'll never see you again.'

'Come, child,' he said, 'I cannot run away from Death. If Death comes for me then there's nothing I can do about it. Come, let me walk you to your mummy.'

And he walked her a little way to the village. She ran crying to her mother.

The old woodcutter walked home and sat there for a little while, and he thought to himself, 'I've had a good life. I've spent a lot of time in the forest, I've seen death in many forms, and if Death's coming for me there's nothing I can do about it. But I'm not going to die hungry. I think I'll make myself a little pot of soup.'

So he got a little skillet and he cut up some vegetables, put them in the skillet to boil and said to himself, 'Soup by its own is not much good. I'll make myself a little bit of bread to go with my soup before Death arrives.'

He always had a bowl, and he filled it full of flour, broke an egg and some milk and some soda and he stirred it up, made a little heap of round dough and put it in the oven to cook.

He's sitting there, didn't even light his pipe, when lo and behold the next thing he heard was 'knock-knock-knock-knock' on the door. And the old woodcutter went to the door. There standing was the stranger, Death, dressed in black with his pale face and bright glassy eyes, his hands by his side.

The woodcutter said, 'I've been expecting you; you may come in!'

And Death walked in. The little stool he sat down on and held his long pale hands to the fire.

And then he spoke for the first time. 'Woodcutter, I have come to visit you to let you understand.'

'My little granddaughter has told me,' he said. 'You scared the child.'

'I did not mean to scare the child,' said Death. 'I have nothing against the child. I just came to see you.' And then he said a strange thing. 'Do I smell soup?' said Death.

The woodcutter said, 'You do. I've just made myself a little pot of soup.'

And Death said, 'Is there enough for two?'

And the old woodcutter said, 'Of course, there's always

enough for two, my friend,' and he took a little bowl, filled it full of soup and passed it across to Death, and filled a little bowl for himself.

And then Death said, 'I also smell fresh bread.'

The old woodcutter said, 'There is fresh bread,' and he opened the oven, took a little loaf which he had cooked not bigger than a big roll and he broke it in half, gave one half to Death and a half to himself.

And he and Death sat there and Death finally cleaned the bowl with the last crust of bread and said, 'Woodcutter, I enjoyed that. Now, it's time to go.' The old woodcutter stood up and reached for his coat, and then Death said, 'Are you going some place, woodcutter?'

The woodcutter says, 'Yes, I'm going with you, you are Death and you've come for me, haven't you?'

And if there were such a thing as a smile and Death could smile, there was a faint smile across Death's face, that pale face.

He shook his head and said, 'No, old woodcutter, I have not come for you. I have come for an old lady in the village who has been in pain and agony for many years and can stand her suffering no more. I have come to take all her pain and suffering away, and give her peace to the end of time. Oh, woodcutter, I knew that you were the only person who understood me and why I have to do what I have to do, so that you and many people like you can survive, and so that people who suffer in pain and agony shall suffer in pain and agony no more. Oh, I'll be coming back for you someday, woodcutter, but it won't be for a long time to come.' And like that Death was gone.

The old woodcutter sat there for a long time. Finally he lighted his pipe and a big smile crossed his face.

He thought to himself, 'What a wonderful story I will have to tell little Mary when she comes to see me next weekend!'

White Pet

This is a wee story about animals; humans have no big part in the story.

When White Pet was born in the month of April many years ago, his mother was awfully sick, and she was a Highland ewe in the west of Scotland. He was very, very weak when he was born, and his mother was so weak that she died a few hours after his birth. When the farmer went out round his sheep one day he came across this wee lamb and it was just standing – it could stand and no more. And he saw its mother lying dead beside it.

He said, 'Poor wee cratur', I'm sorry for you, you're such a delicate wee thing. I think I'll bring you back with me to the farm.' So he picked the wee lamb up – it was only hours old. 'I'll send the ploughman up to bury your mother in the morning.' And he took it home.

When home he comes with it his wife says to him, 'What's that you've got there?'

'It's a wee lamb – poor wee cratur – it would have done as well to die with its mother, I don't think it will survive.'

She says, 'Give it to me – bring it in here and put it beside the fire and I'll see if I can make up a bottle of milk for it – he might survive. If it does he will do for a pet to the wean.'

So she made it a bottle of milk. She got one of the bairn's

teats, from the bottles it had when it was younger, filled a bottle of milk and gave it to the wee lamb. The wee lamb sucked it up.

So they thought the lamb was going to die that night – but no, the next morning he was still alive but so weak he could hardly stand. So the wife put it in a basket beside the fire.

And their wee daughter came home from school; when she saw this wee lamb she was so excited.

She said, 'Daddy, I want that lamb!'

'Well,' he says, 'you can have it.'

So from there on White Pet became the family pet, and he stayed in the family for years and years and years. Ach, he must have stayed in the family for ten or twelve years until the daughter grew up. And he was a pure nuisance round about the farm. He got into everything – but the farmer began to get fed up with him with all the trouble he was getting into.

So one day he said to the wife, 'That lamb is getting into an awful lot of trouble. The lassie's grown too big now and she's no more time for it. I think we'll sell him and put him away with the rest of the sheep.' (This is where the story really begins.)

White Pet was at the back kitchen window and he'd heard this. He said to himself, 'I've been here a long long time and I've spent many happy days here. But they're not going to sell me – I'm not going to have this! Before I get sold and go away somewhere to some other place, I think I'll pack up and clear out and go where nobody can get me.'

So like that he goes up and opens the gate; he'd seen the farmer open the gate many a time – it just had a latch – puts his mouth to the latch and out he goes, shuts the gate behind him and goes on the road. He travels and travels and travels in through this forest for days. He gets tired and he lies down at the roadside.

But he hadn't lain down very long when he heard movements, something coming along the road. And he looked, and there was an old grey donkey. So the lamb naturally was glad to see the old donkey in this forest because he was lonely and he needed the company.

'Good morning,' he says, 'Donkey.'

'Good morning,' Donkey says.

'What puts you in a place like this?' asks White Pet.

'Oho,' he says, 'that's a long story! After all the years that I spent on the farm carting for my master, taking all his vegetables to the village, I was just round in back of the cottage last night when I heard the man and his wife saying I was getting too old and they needed to get a young donkey to take my place. And he would take me and sell me to the first person – probably put me to the knackery.'

'Well,' said the lamb, 'you must be the same as me. I was reared up on a farm and I had a nice mistress, a young farmer's daughter looked after me well. But as the years went by – it was all right when I was wee and she was wee – but as I grew older and she grew older we seemed to drift apart and she had no more time for me. And after she lost interest in me and the farmer lost interest in me, the last night he naturally turned round and told the wife, "We'll have to put him away with the sheep to the market." And I couldn't take that so I cleared out.'

'Well,' said the donkey, 'seeing that we met under these circumstances, I think the best thing you and I can do is pack up, go together as companions and find a place for ourselves where nobody can bother us.'

'Well,' says White Pet, 'I'm quite agreeable if you're agreeable.'

'Okay,' says the donkey, 'so tomorrow morning – we'll

stay here the night and we'll set off tomorrow morning. We'll go well into the forest where nobody can find us, and we can live in peace and contentment for the rest of our days.'

'Okay,' says White Pet the lamb.

So they lay down beneath this tree together and they slept the night out, and the next morning they got up and set sail on the road through this forest. But they hadn't gone half a mile when the first thing they saw was a goose. And this goose was stepping out in the forest all on its own, its neck stretched out, and it was going on and on and on.

'Good morning, Goose,' said White Pet.

'Good morning, Sheep,' said the goose.

'Good morning,' said the donkey.

'And what puts you two on the road at this time of the morning?' said the goose.

'Oho,' White Pet said, 'that's a long, long story! What about you, Goose, what happened to you?'

'Hmm, me? You know, my story's a long, long story too. I had five brothers and five sisters, all reared in the one nest on the one farm. And me, being delicate and young, I wasn't able to take care of myself. The farmer and his wife took me as a pet and reared me up and I stayed with them for years. And the humans round about the place used to get in my road and made me wicked. I used to run and bite at their legs and they said I got to be a nuisance. So last night, just about bedtime, I was sitting out sheltering at the back of the farm when I heard the farmer tell his wife that I was no more use, that the best thing he could do was to send me to the butcher. So, here I am! And I said, "Before I'd go to the butcher I'll pack up and go on my way and find a place where I can stay myself in peace and contentment."'

'Well,' say the lamb and the donkey, 'the same thing happened to us. So if you're game, and you're willing, we're on our way to find a place for ourselves where no humans can bother us in the forest – and I see that you're in the same boat as us – you can mate up with us if you like.'

'Well,' said the goose, 'I'm willing.'

So on they go on their way: the goose in the lead, the lamb next and the donkey following after. They walked on and on and on through the forest but they hadn't walked any more than two or three miles when the first thing they saw coming around this corner was a large cockerel, a great big brown cockerel. The cockerel saw them coming and he stood up as they came up to him.

'Good morning, Goose,' he said. 'Good morning, Lamb; good morning, Donkey. What put you three on the road this time in the morning? You know, I'm only just wakened and I'm an early riser!'

'I can see that,' said the donkey, 'you're an early riser. But we've got a long story to tell.'

'Aha, so have I!' said the cockerel. 'I have a long story to tell . . . and you can hear it if you like.'

'Well,' said the donkey, 'we've come a long way, and if you've got time to listen to our story we have time to listen to yours.'

So they all sat down and the cockerel tells them the story: 'I had a wife and a lot of family and I had a nice place on the farm. And the fox came, he killed my wife and he killed all my family, left nothing but me. Then last night I heard the farmer telling his wife, "If that had been a good cockerel – and we've had him for so many years – and if he'd no have been so feared and had put up a better battle and frightened the fox, all our hens and chickens would be alive today. So the best thing we can do is sell him and get another one in his place." I couldn't take that and I packed up and said, "I'll go on my own road, and find a place for myself where

I'll find peace and quietness away from all human beings."'

'Well,' says the donkey, 'the same thing happened to me.'

'And the same thing to me,' says the lamb.

'And the same thing to me,' says the goose. 'So we've palled up to go our own way, and if you're willing, you can join us.'

'I am,' says the cockerel, 'I am willing. But you know, I'm a very smart walker, and if you don't mind you might let me take the lead along the path!'

'Well,' says the goose, 'it's all right with me.'

'It's all right with me,' says the lamb.

'It's all right with me,' says the donkey.

So the cock goes out in front, stepping out; then comes the goose, then comes the lamb and the donkey comes behind, and they're on their way through the forest. So they walked and they walked and they walked most of the day. They came to this clearing in the forest and there were lovely oak trees spread with plenty of acorns. So the goose and the cockerel had their contentment. And the grass was lovely and green and there was a nice wee brook coming down by, and the lamb and the donkey had their contentment.

'Isn't this a lovely place to stay?' says the lamb.

'It is,' says the goose.

'It is,' says the donkey, 'but what will we do for shelter?'

'Ah,' says the cock, 'there are plenty of trees for me to stay in up here. But I don't fancy it some way. Let us go on a wee bit further before night-time – it'll no be dark for a wee while yet, let's move on a wee bit and see what we can see as long as we're well away from human beings.'

'Right,' says the donkey.

'Right,' says the goose.

'Okay by me,' says the lamb.

'Right,' says the cockerel, 'on we go!'

So they travelled on for another half day till they came to this path leading into the centre of the forest, and by this time it was getting dark. And they saw this hut and there's a light at the window.

The donkey says, 'There are human beings in that hut . . . robbers – who else but robbers in a place like this!'

'I believe you're right,' says the lamb.

Says the cockerel, 'I'll tell you what we can do: if we could get rid of them we could stay here – it's just a lovely place – look at the lovely grass and look at the trees with the acorns!'

'This would suit me,' says the goose, 'I can always paddle in that nice wee brook there.'

'And it would suit me,' says the lamb. 'But first, we must get rid of the robbers.'

'Well,' says the cockerel, 'I'll tell you what to do: we must scare them out of the hut – never to show their faces back in the forest again!'

'Well,' says the donkey, 'how will we do it?'

'Well, I'll tell you,' says the lamb, 'I'm about the cutest one among you because I've had more to do with humans than you, and I used to stay a lot in the house while you were all outside, and I used to listen to a lot of things. So I think I know a wee bit more than you.'

'Well,' says the donkey, 'I'm game.'

'And me,' says the goose. 'I never spent much time in the house to hear what the humans are like.'

'Nor me,' says the cockerel.

The lamb says, 'Look, I'll tell you what to do: I'll go to the window and I'll shout through the window. And,' he says to the cockerel, 'you climb up to the top of the roof and you make a carry-on, the biggest racket you can when I start! And,' he says to the goose, 'you do the same at the door!

And,' he says to the donkey, 'you stay – when the door opens you turn your back to the door and every time that one comes out, hit them a good-going kick!'

So they all made up their plan to do this. The cockerel flew up to the top of the hut; nobody heard him. The lamb goes round, this big white-faced woolly lamb goes round to the window. (In these days there was no glass in the window or anything, just a window and a piece of skin or the like hanging on it.) The donkey takes his place up at the front door. And so does the goose.

So the lamb pulls back the window cloth and he keeks in – there are three robbers sitting at a big fire inside the hut, this wooden hut. So he passes the word around and he tells the others.

Then he goes to the window and shouts, 'Baaaa!' in through the window. And the robbers look out – they see this white face.

Then the cockerel's on the top of the roof – 'Cock-a-doodle-doo!'

And the goose at the door goes, 'Hsssssst!' and makes the biggest racket you've ever heard!

With the fright the robbers got they opened the door and all ran out, and as every one ran out the donkey just gave them a kick one after the other, knocked them all scattering! The robbers got such a fright, they ran and ran and ran. And this donkey and the lamb and the goose and the cockerel kept up so much of a racket that the robbers could still hear them at a distance. When they came to the clearing they were fairly puffed out – they stopped.

One said to the other, 'What was *that* that came in there?'

'I don't know,' said the other one, 'but I'll tell you something, there's something funny happened in that place – I'll never go back!'

'Nor me,' said the other one.

'Nor me,' said the second one. 'What did *you* see? I heard the devil on the roof shouting, "Send him up to me, send him up to me!"'

'And,' the third one says, 'there was a large snake at the door and it was hissing, and a ghost at the window was shouting through, and a giant with a club – as soon as I came out he hit me a welt and knocked me scattering!'

So the three robbers say, 'The best thing we can do is pack up and never go back near that place again!'

After that everything quietened down. The lamb, the goose, the donkey and the cockerel all went into the hut and they sat and talked it over.

'We'll stay here,' says the lamb, 'this is a fine place for us.'

'And,' the cockerel said, 'I'll take my place at night on the roof, I'll be the watchman.'

'I'll stay by the door,' says the goose, 'and I'll be a watchman.'

'And I'll lie down by the fire,' said the lamb, 'where I always used to.'

'And I'll lie outside the door,' says the donkey, 'and use my hooves on anything that comes about. I don't think we'll ever be troubled by human beings again.'

So they stayed in that place in the forest till the end of their days.

And that is the last of the story.

I heard another version of this story while I was at school, but 'White Pet' was told by different Travellers around their campfires and this is the way they knew it.

The Goat that Told Lies

This was a most fantastic story among the Travellers and it has passed through the travellers by word of mouth, as far as I know, for some four hundred years, maybe more – from when the Travellers began. When Travelling people gathered around the campfire and the children were a wee bit annoying to their mothers and fathers, one of the fathers would say, 'Come on, I'll tell you a story!' to keep the children quiet. The children would gather round and he would say, 'What will I tell you?' And they would say, 'Daddy, tell us about the goat, the goat that told lies.' I hope you will enjoy the story, as these little children who are grandfathers and grandmothers by this time, and some of them dead long ago, were reared and brought up on this tale. And I hope this story will go on for ever and ever, not only among the Traveller children, but among all people who are really interested.

Many years ago, long before your day and mine, there lived a woodcutter in the forest and he had three sons. He and his wife depended on what little money they could make from cutting the trees in the forest but they had a contract with the laird that they wouldn't cut any green trees, only what was blown down with the wind, or dead wood. This old man and his sons used to go into the forest every morning and cut all this wood and they didn't have a pony to take the wood from the forest, they hurled it with a handcart. It was a long way into the forest but the sons, Willie, Jack, and Thomas, loved their father and mother dearly and helped them every way they could.

From where they stayed it was about a ten-mile hike to the village. The old man used to take the handcart and hurl all the sticks he had cut and sell them in the village for money. And once a month they used to go to the village for their rations, the groceries they needed to keep themselves, to survive in the forest.

The story really begins one morning, before the old man and his three sons went into the forest.

The old man got up and had his breakfast, and he said to his old wife, 'Well, Maggie, we'll have to go again today and I think we'll be gone for a while.'

'Well,' she said, 'you know it's lonely for me being here by myself all day. I wish I had something to keep me in company – a dog or a cat, anything. Something to talk to.'

'Och,' he said, 'don't worry. You'll be all right. If we get a quick load we'll be back early.' But the father and the three sons went on their way to the forest.

They had a good distance to walk and when they landed at their work place in the forest the father said, 'The best thing we can do is split up: Willie, you go that way; Tommy, you go that way; and Jack, you go this way. And if you come to any dead trees, just knock them down, put them in a heap and we'll collect them later.'

So the boys said, 'All right!' to their father and away they went into the forest.

But the old man had chosen a part of the forest he had never been in before and he walked forward. He saw some dead trees and he said, 'Probably I'll get a better one further on,' and he walked further in and further in. He came to this large tree – it was dead right to the top. And he had his axe with him, he was ready to cut it, when right at the foot of the tree he saw this thing. It was a baby goat, a young kid. And the old man stopped, he looked.

'Well,' he said, 'upon my soul! Where in the name of God do you come from, little creature – where did you come from?'

'He-eh,' the goat said, 'ha-a-haah, where did I come from – that's a long story.'

And the old man looked all around as if there was somebody else there. But he saw there was nobody. He felt kind of funny.

He said, 'Did that animal speak or am I hearing things?' He rubbed his ears.

The goat said, 'Look, Johnnie,' (he called the old man Johnnie) 'you mightnae rub your ears or look for anybody else here in the forest – there's nobody here but me.'

He says, 'Goat, do you speak?'

And the goat said, 'Aye, I speak. But I only speak to folk that I like! And I know about you and your wife and your three sons, and I know how you come to the forest every day.'

The old man was mesmerized; he didn't know what to do. He said, 'Never in my life did I hear a goat speaking!'

'But,' the goat said, 'dinnae think I'm going to speak to your three sons! What kind of a woman is your wife?'

'O-oh,' Johnnie said, 'my wife is the nicest old cratur – I've been married to her for sixty years and she's the nicest old woman that God ever put on this earth.'

'Ah,' the goat said, 'that's good! I like that.'

'Well,' he said, 'I can't leave you here. I think I'll take you back with me. My old wife needs somebody like you to keep her in company.'

'Well . . .' the goat says, 'but I'll tell you something, old man, before you go any further. I know about your three sons – Willie, Jack and Tommy – they're out there in the forest not far from here cutting trees. But don't think I'm going to speak to them because I'm not! I'll speak to you and I'll speak to your old wife, whatever kind of woman she is – I'll make my mind up what kind of person she is when I get there.'

The old man says, 'You're a funny goat. But I like you, I like you a lot.'

'And I like you too,' the goat said, 'I like you a lot. I think I'll just go with you.'

So instead of cutting any sticks the old man picked the goat up under his arm and walked back through the forest. He landed in a clearing in the forest and he met his three sons, and they had all these heaps of sticks packed up.

Willie said, 'Daddy, did you get any sticks?'

'Oh, stop speaking about sticks, son! I got something better than sticks. I've got something for your mother.'

The boys said, 'What is it?'

He said, 'A goat!'

'A goat, father?' they said.

He says, 'A baby goat.' But the old man never said it could speak! 'I got a baby goat, this is the thing your mother's been wanting for years, something to keep her in company. She can feed it and pet it and do what she likes with it while we're out working in the forest.'

So Willie came over. He looked at the goat, and the goat gave him the eye. Jack came over and he looked at the goat, and the goat gave him the eye. And Thomas, the youngest one, came over and he looked at the goat, and the goat didn't look very pleased at him.

'So, I'll tell you what we'll do,' the father said, 'you each take some sticks and carry them home on your backs and I'll carry the goat. We'll go home more the day* to your mother.'

So the three young men carried a load of sticks on their backs and the old man carried the goat. And back home they went. But the old man couldn't wait to get into the house, and while the sons were putting down the sticks he ran round and opened the door.

He said, 'Maggie, Maggie!'

She says, 'What is it, did you cut yourself or something?'

'No, come here! Look what I got for you!' And old Maggie looked. He said, 'I got you a goat.'

She says, 'What?'

'I've got you a goat.'

'But where, in the name of the world,' she said, 'did you get a goat?'

He says, 'Wheeshst! Don't say a word. Don't tell the boys. This is not the kind of goat that you find about any place. Maggie, this is a different kind of goat. This goat can speak!'

'Away! Johnnie, a goat can't speak. A goat can't speak!'

And the goat up and said, 'Aye, Maggie, I can speak. Take me in and give me a wee heat at the fire, I'm kind o' cold.' Oh, old Maggie's eyes popped out of her head.

She says, 'Give me the wee cratur!'

Old Maggie got the goat, took it in her bosom and put it in beside the fire. She gave it a heat and the goat sat down beside the fire. She had the boys' supper made, and the boys came in and had their supper. They were tired. The old man and his wife had their bed downstairs and up the small stair

* more the day – for the rest of the day

to the floor above the three young men had their beds. So the three young men went away to their beds. Now, old Maggie was sitting at one side of the fire, Johnnie was sitting at the other side and the goat was sitting in the middle.

'You know, Maggie,' he said, 'it's a funny thing – I wonder where that wee creature came from?'

The goat was sitting, its ears hanging down, not saying a word.

'Well,' she said, 'you could ask where it came from – ask it!'

He said, 'Maggie, it'll no speak – it'll speak to you, it'll speak to me, but it'll no speak to the laddies. It doesn't want the laddies to know it can speak, and it'll no say a word!'

'Oh well,' she said. 'But Johnnie, what are we going to do with it? I can't leave it in here by the fire all night because sparks might land on it, and it needs to go outside sometimes.'

'Maggie, I'll go out and make a nice wee place in the shed for it.'

So he went out to an old shed that he used to keep for his hens (he had no more hens because they ate them all when they had no more food), and he filled it full of straw and hay and he got a nice pail of water and he made a nice wee bed for the goat. And he put her down.

'Now,' he said, 'you sleep there, wee cratur, and we'll take good care of you.'

'Thank you, Johnnie, you're awfae kind,' the goat said. 'And tell old Maggie I'll see her in the mornin'.'

So the old man went in.

She said, 'Did you take care of the goat?'

'Oh,' he said, 'I took care of the goat, and it thanked me awful much.'

'What did it say to you?'

`It said, "Thank you, Johnnie, thank you very much for

being so good to me, and tell old Maggie I'll see her in the morning." '

'All right,' said old Maggie, 'I'll see it in the morning all right!'

So the old couple went away to their bed. But old Maggie couldn't rest thinking about this goat. She spoke about this goat.

She said, 'Johnnie, it's just the thing I need here all day with me – it'll keep me in company, I can take it into the house with me and I can feed it and I can look after it and I can brush it and take care of it. While you're away – I'll no miss you away in the forest all day now I have somebody to speak to!'

So the next day old John and his three sons go away to the forest and Maggie spends her time with the goat. She and the goat become the greatest of friends. She cuddles it, kisses it, does everything with it.

'Wee cratur,' she said, 'I'll be good to you.' And she called it Nellie. 'Nellie, I'll look after you.'

'Well, old wife,' she says, 'I'll love my life here with you and old Johnnie, but I'm no so keen on those laddies. I doubt they would be bad to me if they got a chance. They don't look at me very pleasantly – I don't like the looks of them. I don't . . .'

'Oh,' she said, 'my laddies are all right, they wouldn't hurt a hair on your body – it wouldn't pay them either to hurt a hair on your body. If I got them lifting a hand to you it'd be the cause of their death!'

So from that day on Maggie and the goat became the greatest friends in the world. She loved it from her heart, and because she loved it and old John loved her, he loved the goat as much as he loved old Maggie. And every night when the boys went to their beds he carried Nellie in to the fire, where he put her down. Nellie sat and she cracked to them, she told them stories and tales, she told them everything – but she never said where she came from. Not a word did she tell them about where she came from.

But, to make a long story short, it came time when somebody had to go to the village for messages. By this time Nellie had begun to grow, and she was a good-sized, half-grown goat. The father called all his sons together that night after the hard day's work was finished.

'Boys, we're kind of short of food. And I need tobacco and your mother needs some things from the village. Tomorrow I want one of you to go to the village and bring back some messages, whatever your mother needs.'

And old Maggie said, 'Aye, and you'll take wee Nellie with you to the village for a walk because she's been tied up here all day at home with me while you've been away. I've made a belt for her and a nice collar – you'll take her with you for a walk to the town! And upon my soul, be good to her! Don't walk her feet on the hard road, keep her on the grass and stop along the way and give her a good drink. Treat her like you would treat your own mother!'

So Willie said, 'Mother, I wouldn't hurt your wee goat, I know you love it – though I don't like it!'

Now the goat hated these boys – it was jealous of them! It didn't like them at all. The next morning came.

Willie got up, got his breakfast, got money from his mother and he got a bag. He went into the shed, took the goat by the rope, and led the goat into the village. He walked it on the grass and he stopped along the way, he gave it a drink of water and he fed it and he took his time with it, bought it apples from the shop – and he treated it like a queen, all the way to the village and all the way back!

After he came home, before he even took the messages

into his mother, he took the goat into the shed, tied it up, made it a bed of soft straw, got a nice pail of water and put it down beside the goat. Then he went in for his supper, gave his mother his messages and his father his tobacco. They sat and talked for a while, they asked him about the village and he said that everything was okay there. And Willie went away upstairs to his bed. So the old mother and father sat and talked for a wee while.

'Johnnie,' she says, 'I think you should go and bring wee Nellie in for a while. I'm wearying to see her, I haven't seen her all day. And put her down by the fire where I can see her.'

The boys were upstairs in their beds. It was about twelve o'clock at night and the old man was sitting smoking his pipe at the fire and old Maggie was sitting in her chair.

'Well, I will go out and bring wee Nellie in,' he said, 'she must be feeling kind o' cold out there! I'll bring her in for a wee heat.'

So out he went and brought in the goat. They had a sheepskin rug at the front of the fire. He put the goat at the front of the fire.

She said, 'How are you feeling the night*, Nellie?'

'Oh woman, dinnae speak to me,' she said, 'dinnae speak to me!'

'What's wrong with you?'

'Oh-oh,' she says, 'what's wrong wi' me? You've nae idea what's wrong wi' me – that laddie o' yours . . .'

'What's wrong with that laddie,' she says, 'what did he do?'

'Do to me?' she said. 'Oh, you've no idea what he's done to me – he kicked me and he battered me and I never had a bite today and he *pulled* me on the rope as hard as he could, and

---

* the night - tonight

my poor feet are that sore I can hardly stand up! And when he got to the village he tied me up to a wall where I couldn't get a bite and he put wee weans on my back for pennies, and gave them a hurl. And my poor back's that sore I can't even move!'

The old man said, 'Nellie, are you telling the truth?'

The goat said, 'I'm telling the God's honest truth, why would I tell you a lie, to you people who are so good to me? That's what your son has done to me, that laddie! That son you've got – he's a beast, he's an animal!'

'Well,' the old man said, 'it'll never happen again in this house. Tomorrow morning, when he comes down that stair, I'm going to make him so that he'll never again be cruel to his mother's wee pet!'

True to his word, the old man got up the first thing in the morning, and before he got breakfast – never even tied his boots – when his son came down the stair (Willie always came down first because he was the oldest one), he took a walking stick from behind the door and gave Willie the biggest beating he ever had in his life. He laid into him for an hour.

'Now,' he said, 'go on your way and never show your face back here about this house as long as you live! Don't ever come back! You cruel boy who was cruel to your mother's wee pet – the only thing she has to keep her in company!'

Willie was sent on his way never to be seen again. So the two brothers were kind of sad at losing their brother because they liked to be together. Now, there was more animosity towards the goat – they hated the goat worse for this! But they didn't know what happened because their mother and father never told them. They worked hard with their father just the same and a month passed by and it was once again time to go to the shop for their messages.

Now it was Jack's turn, the next brother. And he did the same thing. But if Willie was good to the goat, Jack was ten times better. He half-carried it to the town and half-carried it back! He bought cookies and he bought scones for it and he fed it on flowers along the way and gave it a drink of water, and did everything he could possibly do for the goat – but no, it was no good. He gave his mother the messages, gave his father his tobacco, sat and had his supper and went upstairs to bed.

She said, 'Johnnie, I don't know – that laddie, he might have been bad to that wee goat today – you'd better go and bring it in and see what it's got to say the night!'

Old Jock goes out for the goat, brings it in, puts it down by the fire. The goat, she's stretched out.

'How are you feeling the night, Nellie?'

'O-oh,' she says, 'don't speak to me, woman, I can't talk, I can't talk to you – I'm too sore. That laddie o' yours took revenge on me and he kicked me the whole way to the town and he kicked me the whole way back. I'm so sick I can't even move, so dinnae speak nae mair tae me! I just want to lie doon. And please! Don't put me back in that shed the night – can you let me lie by the fire?'

The old man said, 'God bless us, that's terrible! You poor wee beast! But wait, upon my soul, he's no getting off with it – tomorrow morning when he comes down that stair, I'm going to make him so that he'll never treat you badly again, Nellie! Don't worry – you'll no need to worry about him.'

So the next morning, true to his word, the old man – before he even got breakfast – when Jack came down the stair, he laid into Jack with the walking stick. And if he gave Willie a beating he gave Jack a bigger beating.

And he said, 'Look, *you* follow your brother and never

show your face about my house as long as you live! You *cruel* laddie, what you did to your mother's wee beast!' So Jack was sent on his way, the same as his brother.

Now there were only the father and Tommy left. Tommy was kind of fed up and he hated the goat worse by this time because he knew there was something wrong.

He said, 'My brothers couldn't be bad to that goat. My brothers never hurt anybody, and how did they know anyway – the goat can't speak, the goat can't tell them anything.' This is what Tommy said to himself, 'Well, I'll tell you one thing, if it comes my chance to take it to the town, I'm not going to be bad to it! I don't want to leave my father and mother and I have no place to go.' And he worried about this, you see.

But another month passed by and it came to Tommy's turn, and the same thing happened to him. If the two brothers were good to the goat, Tommy was ten times better. He treated it even more like a queen! He picked wee soft flowers and put them on the grass and patted wee Nellie.

'Now you be a good wee goat and come with me, and I'll look after you, and don't worry,' said Tommy. He did all the things he could for the goat on the way to the village and on the way back – bought it sweeties and he fed it sweeties. He came back, put her in the shed, filled a nice pail of water and made a nice wee bed for her. 'Lie down there and keep yourself warm, wee Nellie,' he said.

He went in, had his supper and went to his bed. The old mother and father, old Johnnie and old Maggie, were sitting at the fireside.

She said, 'Johnnie, I wonder how wee Nellie's getting on. I'd like to see her before I go to bed,' because this old woman loved the goat from her heart.

'Oh well, I'll bring her in for a wee while,' he said, 'it's getting kind o' cold, it's getting near the wintertime now and probably she'd be better to sleep by the fire tonight.'

He brought the goat in and put it down by the fire. And the goat just lay down, stretched its legs out – couldn't move.

And old Maggie said, 'How are you feeling the night, wee Nellie?'

'O-o-oh, dear-dear woman!' she said, 'I can't speak to you, I can't speak! Don't ask me questions – I'm just about finished, I don't think I'll see the night out! I think I'm finished for good!'

'What's wrong with you?'

'Oh, that laddie of yours,' she said, 'he killed me, he finally finished me. What his two brothers didn't do, he finally did it. I'm just about finished, I'll never see daylight – I'll never see the morning!'

And the old woman started to greet. And when the old woman started to greet the old man felt so sad.

'I'm no waiting till morning,' he said, 'I'm going to get him right now!'

So he goes up the stair and pulls young Thomas out of bed and gives him the biggest beating he ever got in his life and sends him – in the darkness – off! Never to show his face again.

The goat heard this and the goat said, `Haa! That's the last of them. Thank God, that's the last of them gone! Now it's just me and old Johnnie and Maggie and I'll enjoy my life here with them two.'

It sprung up to its feet and sat right at the front of the fire. It sat and it joked and it told cracks and stories to the old man and the old woman till the old man and woman felt sleepy.

And old Maggie says, 'Nellie, my doll, I'll have to go to bed more the night. I've enjoyed this night, this is the best night that ever I had in my life! Will you be all right, Nellie?'

'A-aye,' she said, 'old woman, I'll be all right!'

'How are you feeling, is your body still sore?'

'Ach, I'm no so bad noo,' she said, 'since I had a wee crack to youse and I'm feeling a wee bit better, I'll probably be all right by the morning.'

So the old man and the old woman kissed the goat, cuddled it and bade it good-night. 'You'll stay by the fire the night, Nellie?'

'I'll stay by the fire, old wife,' she said, 'and I'll be all right.'

So the old man and woman went away to bed. And she said, 'Johnnie, I can never thank you, never thank you enough for what you've done for me getting me that wee goat. I love my wee goat!'

'Old wife,' he said, 'look, I love you. And anybody who'd be bad to your wee goat, I wouldn't have any time for them – even my own sons. But I'll tell you something, I'm going to miss the laddies. But they'll have to learn to go their own way. If they'd been good to your wee goat, they wouldn't have got what they got. And it's me and you and Nellie from now on. I'll manage by cutting sticks, I'll manage myself to get as much as will keep me and you alive. As long as you've got wee Nellie to keep you in company.'

So, the goat was happy. The old man was happy, and the old woman was happy, but they missed the laddies. But the old man was true to his word, he worked hard and he worked away for a month. And the goat was in with old Maggie every day in the week and she and the goat spent a fantastic time! She loved the goat so much she just couldn't bear to have it out of her sight. But things began to get short, they had no food and it came the time that somebody had to go the the village.

And the old man said, 'Well, you can't go, old Maggie. I'll go to the village, and I'll take wee Nellie with me. I'll no be bad to her. Whatever's going in the town, she gets half of it – everything I buy, she gets half.'

So, true to his word, the next morning the old man got up bright and early, and before he got breakfast he went out and brought the goat in.

'Come on now, Nellie, sit by the fire and have a wee heat,' he said, 'and have a wee crack to the old wife there because me and you are going to the town today, and I'll get you something bonnie. What do you like?'

'Oh well, I'm fond of sweeties and I like pancakes and I like scones and,' she says, 'anything that's kind of sweet.'

'I'll get you plenty of sweet things, Nellie, don't worry,' he said. 'I'm, not like these laddies, I'll no be bad to you.' So he said to the old woman, 'Give me some extra money to get something for Nellie. She and I will go to town.'

So the old man got Nellie by the rope and a bag on his back, and away he went. And if the three boys were good to Nellie, the old man was ten times better. He treated her like a baby, all the way to the town and on the way back he treated her the same! When he came back, he put her into the shed – before he even had a bite to eat himself – made a nice wee bed of straw for her, got her a nice pail of clean water.

And he said, 'Nellie, you lie down there and keep yourself warm. When I get a bite to eat I'll bring you in to the fire to see the old wife.'

And the goat lay down. Now the goat never said anything. It wasn't very happy.

So he came in, he gave his old wife all the messages, she made a nice supper for the old man and he lay back, lighted his pipe, untied his boots.

And she said, 'Johnnie, before you take your boots off, would you bring wee Nellie in?'

'Aye! I'll go and get Nellie now! She'll tell you how good I was to her. I'm no like your sons, I'm no bad-hearted.' He goes, carries in the goat, and puts it down in the front of the fire.

'Well, Nellie,' old Maggie said, 'how are you feeling the night?'

'Oh, woman, don't speak to me, how am I feeling – you shouldn't ask these things of me!' she said. 'How could you manage to stay all these years with that animal of a man you've got? That's a beast, that's worse than every son you ever had. The laddies were bad, but God bless us, that man was worse!' And the old man was sitting at the fire. 'He kicked me and he battered me and he blamed me for his sons. When he got me away from your house a wee bit, he put all his ill will on me because his sons weren't there to help him, and he nearly killed me dead! And I'm no able to move. I cannae talk to you – let me lie doon by your fire!'

'Ah!' said the old man, 'so that's the way it is, is it? Well, Nellie, I brought you to this house for the sake of my old wife to keep her in company, but you ruined my sons' lives. I never hurt you in any way but I'm going to hurt you now!' And he caught the goat and he pulled it outside and he got a walking stick. He beat it and he beat it and he beat it, till the goat couldn't move. 'Now,' he said to the goat, 'get on your way and never show your face back about my house again as long as you live! *You unsanctified jeejament animal*! My poor wee laddies treated you the way I treated you and that's the thanks we get.'

So the goat makes off. And on the goat goes, travels on and travels on.

And he went back in. 'Woman!'

She said, 'What did you do to wee Nellie?'

He says, 'I did to Nellie what Nellie needed. Woman, that's an evil beast! All that time when me and you were thinking the world of it . . . I never hurt it, I never touched it on the way to the village!'

And the old woman believed him, she believed her old man because she knew he was telling the truth. She kent him through and through.

He said, 'I treated it like a baby and you heard what it said to me. I bet you a pound to a penny the laddies did the same thing, and I gave my wee sons a beating and sent them off – God knows where they are now – for nothing, over the head of that beast, *that animal*, that unsanctified goat!' He said, 'Nothing good will come out of it!'

And the old woman said, 'Johnnie, I believe you, I believe you because there's no goat could speak anyway – unless it was evil. God knows where my wee laddies are.' The old woman started to greet.

The old man said, 'Never mind, maybe we'll come across your laddies sometime.'

But we'll leave the old people now and we'll go with the goat.

The goat travels on, it travels on, travels on all night, right through the forest till it comes to the sea. And the heavy waves were lashing against the shore, and it's looking for a place to sleep. A goat's a good climber, and it climbs up the face of this cliff and comes to a nice wee cave in the cliff-face. It goes in, it lies down in the cave. And oh, it's sore, its body is sore with the beating the old man gave it. And its feet are sore with walking so far.

It's saying, 'O-oh dear-oh dear-oh dear, I'm sore! Ooh my feet, my feet, my body. O-oh dear, what did I do this for! Was I no better back with my old woman, lying among straw and getting petted by the fire? What in the name of God was I thinking about, why have I been so stupid and so foolish?' And the goat's talking away to itself and it's moaning with the pain.

But unknown to the goat a fox had its den in this cave and it had two wee cubs at the very back, and they were lying among a wee puckle straw that the fox had brought in. Now this mother fox had been away hunting all night for something for the cubs to eat. She had caught a rabbit. And by the time she had got back it was daylight. It was the summertime and the sun was shining. When she came back to the cave she heard this noise from within.

'O-oh dear-oh dear-oh dear I'm sore! O-o-o-oh-o-oh-o-oh me-me, what did I do this for?'

The vixen was afraid to go in. She said, 'It must be the devil in there! I can't go in there, and my two wee babies are going to die with the hunger – I can't go in to them!'

And she's sitting greeting with the wee rabbit in front of her, sitting in front of the cave. And the goat's still carrying on and moaning away with the pain, when who comes by but a bumble-bee.

And he goes, 'bvizzzzz,' hunting for flowers. And the bumble-bee was well acquainted with the fox, so he buzzes around two or three times, 'bvizzzzzzzzz,' and lands beside the fox. The bumble-bee says, 'What's wrong, Fox?'

'O-oh wheesht!' the fox said. 'In there – the devil – in that cave! My two babies are in there and I've got a wee bite here for them, a wee rabbit I managed to catch. I've been all night looking for it and I can't go in! Listen,' she said to the bumble-bee, 'listen! The devil – it's in there!'

And the goat's lying. 'O-o-oh-me-o-o-o-oh, I'm sore-I'm sore, I'll never see daylight, I'll never see the morning! Oh my poor legs and my poor feet, o-oh, curse upon that old man and curse upon his sons, curse upon his old woman – they've done this to me!'

The bumble-bee went in, flew round about, and he saw the goat lying on its side. He came back out.

He said to the fox, 'Don't worry, I'll help you. Just hang on, just sit there! I'll no be long till I'm back.' And away the bumble-bee goes, 'hmmmmmmmmmm,' two hundred miles an hour! Away he goes back to the hive, he lands in the hive and says to all his friends, 'Look! You've been hanging about this hive all day, you've never done very much, now come with me, I've got a job for you! Come with me!' said the bumble-bee. 'I need you very quickly. Sharpen your stings!'

And all the bumble-bees say, 'Right, we'll go with you!'

So they all landed back at the cave, about seventeen hundred bumble-bees – nearly two thousand! And they stopped. The fox was still sitting.

'Now,' says the bumble-bee, 'in there! And where you hear a noise – moaning and groaning going on – sting to your hearts' content! Sting hard and sting strong.'

So in go the bumble-bees, and one after the other they stung the goat. They stung the goat, every part of it. And the goat got such a fright – it went straight out of the cave with the pain of the stings! And when it came out, it forgot it was on a cliff and went right out, into the sea, and was drowned. It never was heard of again, never heard of!

And the fox went in to its wee babies, gave them the

rabbit; and the bees went back to the hive. And that's the end of the goat – and that's the end of my story!

My daddy used to tell us this one; aye, he told us this dozens of times. I always liked that one and it was one of his favourites too.

The Traveller Woman who Looked Back

You see, the Travellers had their own way of telling stories. Take the Bible story of Lot's Wife turned to a pillar of salt: now whether they invented their own story or the story originally started as Lot's wife and then got changed around as they went, I don't know. But this is the story the way it was told to me.

Up near Appin in Argyllshire, by Oban, at a wee camping place beside a loch, there's a stone. It's covered with heather and probably nobody ever pays much attention to it. But if you took a good look at this stone, stood back and admired it, you'd see the picture of an old woman with her wee creel on her arm and a shawl over her shoulders. It's called the Appin Stone, in the form of an old Traveller woman.

Now, the story states that this old Traveller woman and her old man came late on the road at night with a wee handcart, and they had their bits of camping stuff in it. They'd been travelling on and on, and she'd been hawking the houses and the old crofts on their way selling things or trying to get as much as she could. But it was a bad day for both of them! She could get very little. And her old man's name was John. They came to this wee camping place beside the loch.

She said, 'John, I'm tired, I can't go any further.'

He says, 'Woman, we can't stay here. We haven't got a bite – we've nothing to eat, nothing to drink. What are we going to stay here for?'

'Well, I can't go any further,' she said, 'you put up the tent, and I'll go up there through the wood to that house. I see a light in the house – I might get something that'll make a wee bit of supper for me and you for the night.'

'Woman,' he says, 'there's no house up there! I've been this road before, there's the ruins of an old castle – but no house.'

She said, 'Look! It's all lighted up! It's bene hantle, it's gentry there for the shooting.'

'No, woman,' he says, 'it's no! That's the ruin of an old castle up there, just ruins – maybe four walls and that's all that's in it.'

'Who are you trying to make a fool of!' she said. 'You get the tent up and I'll go up to the castle. There may be maids – I could maybe read their hands or tell fortunes or something. I'll maybe get some tea and sugar and maybe a drop of milk, something to make a bite for me and you for the night.'

'Well, well, if you see a light, you go! I'll put the tent up.'

The old man put his wee tent up. The old woman walked up the path. It was all grown with weeds and thorns, you know, but she made her way up. She said to herself, 'It's kind o' droll that the folk who look after this house don't keep the road in very good order.'

But she could still see the light. She followed on, she wandered up and when she landed – here was the beautiful castle all lighted up! She heard laughing and merriment and dancing coming from within.

'Ah!' she says. 'He kens nothing about it: this is all shooting bene hantle here for the summer holiday! They're bound to give me something!'

She went round with her wee basket to the back door and it was one of thon old-fashioned doors with the iron studs on it and a big knocker. The old woman caught the knocker and gave it two or three rattles, clack, bump, bump-bump – but she never stood two minutes when out came the cook with a white bonnet on his head.

He says, 'What is it, what do you want?'

'Well, look, son,' she called him. 'Me and my old man came late the night, and we're camped down there and we haven't very much to eat. I'll give you something out o' my basket if you could maybe give me something to make our supper for the night.'

He was a very pleasant man. He says, 'Wait a minute, I'll go in and see the Master.'

In he goes. In he goes to the hall where all these young ladies, young gentlemen were all drinking wine and enjoying themselves, singing and dancing and playing cards in the great big hall. He walks up to the Master.

He says, 'Master, there's an old lady at the back door, an old tinker-traveller woman.'

'What does she want?' asks the Master of the house.

'Oh,' he said, 'she wants something to eat.'

He says, 'If she wants something to eat bring her in! Get her in here!'

Away he goes, the cook, back out.

He says to the old woman, 'You have to come in!' The old woman was kind of shanned, she didn't want to go in. She said, 'Son, I don't like going into folk's houses.'

'The Master of the house said if you want anything in here you've got to come in!'

Oh, no way – the woman wouldn't be beat. But she walks into this great big hall. And all these young ladies and young gentlemen, they never paid any attention to her, never looked the road she was on! And sitting on this great big chair in front of this table was this man. Tall – about six foot tall – dark . . . a very handsome man.

'Come over, my old lady!' he said. 'What is it you want?'

'Well . . .' She told him the story.

'Ha-ha!' he said. 'That's true, that's true! Well, bring her a glass of wine!'

So the cook went over and he filled this great big glass of wine and he gave it to the old woman. She drank it up.

He said, 'Is that good?'

'O-o-oh, Master,' she says, 'it's good!'

'Now, you want something to eat, don't you?'

'Yes, I want something to eat,' she says.

'Well, have another glass of wine!' he said. 'And on the way out give the cook your basket. I told him to give you anything you want in your basket.'

She says, 'God bless you, son!'

He said, 'Woman, don't say that word in here – God's not mentioned in here, don't say "God bless me!" But your god *help you tonight*,' he said, '*if you look back here on your road when you leave this place!*'

The old woman felt kind o' droll. She thanked him very much.

'Now,' he says, 'on your way!'

Away goes the old woman with the cook and the cook packs the old woman's basket with everything she needs, everything she requires under the sun. She thanks the cook very much.

'Okay, old wife,' he said, 'on your way – and be careful – watch that road!'

But the old woman went down the road and she said, 'That's queer. That's a shan deekin gadgie*, a nice man, but

* shan deekin gadgie – bad looking, dreadful, man

there's something queer about that folk. Because *all* those people never even looked at me in that hall! They're droll hantle,' she says to her ownself, 'very very droll hantle. The cook never spoke to me very much . . . but that gentleman! He's a funny man – I'll have to tell old Johnnie about him when I go back. He doesn't seem to be bad, but there's somethin' awfae funny about him that I dinnae like – even suppose he gien me plenty meat in the basket.'

So she stopped. And it was all buttony boots they had in these days, the old women wore buttony boots – and they were laced up to below her knee. And didn't her – as she was coming through the brambles and getting near to the camp – didn't her lace come loose with the brambles. She stooped down and she laced her boot. Then she walked on a wee bit . . . but she couldn't resist it – she looked back! And as she looked back the lights went out. In the castle. Out went the lights. . . .

The old man sat. He sat and he waited the whole fairin night. The old woman never came back.

'God bless my soul and body,' he said, 'she went up that path somewhere – up that path somewhere!' But he waited till God's daylight in the morning, till it was the break of day, and he said, 'I'll have to go and see, maybe she fell into a hole or something. I told her not to go in the first place!'

Up he goes. And he walks past the stone – he never sees it! The castle was in ruins, brackens growing in the castle, you know – nothing but the walls and the rest in ruins.

'I told her, that silly old cratur, not to come up here at night-time,' he says, 'she must have fallen in a hole.'

But on the road coming back down he stopped. He looked.

'God bless me,' he said, 'if you weren't made of stone, I'd swear that you were my old wife!'

And there was the old woman with a basket on her arm and the two-three messages* and her wee shawl over her shoulders – solid rock – at the side of the road going to the old man's camp.

So the old man waited for three days, then he reported it to the police and told them the story. 'My old wife said she saw lights in it . . .'

'She might have seen lights in it,' he said. 'Legend said that the *Devil*, that the man who owned that castle was so bad he worked with the Devil. And one night it went on fire, it was burned to the ground. But they never got one single body in the castle – people said that everybody was taken away by the Devil. And,' he said, 'once every hundred years the Devil brings them back there and he has a party! If your old wife joined that party, God knows where she is today!' And the old man never found his old wife. But to this day that pillar of stone is still in the place, there to this day.

And that's the last o' my wee story.

My granny told me that story years and years ago, old Belle MacDonald. I was very young then, but on cold winter nights it was storytelling around the fire in the middle of the floor, just a stick fire in the middle of the tent, a hole in the roof and the smoke going straight up through the hole. A little paraffin lamp, the cruisie turned down, home-made by my father. And Granny would tell a story, then Father would tell a story. . .

---

* two-three messages – food she got

Jack and the Witch's Bellows

Jack and his old mother stayed in this wee house in the village. Jack had a job in a wee shop beside the house and he used to mend bellows for blowing up the fire. Oh, and he made some of the loveliest bellows you ever saw! He bought in his leather and he sorted the bellows: he put new brass points on them, and he carved things on the handles . . . oh, he had a lovely trade! He kept himself and his old mother the best way he could. So his fame for sorting bellows spread all over the country.

But one day he was sitting in his wee shop and was making two or three bellows when his mother shouted through to him, 'Come on, Jack, come on! You're working in there all day. Do you never think of stopping and coming through for a wee bite to eat?'

'I'll be with you in a minute, Mother,' he said.

So, anyway, through he comes. And he and his old mother are sitting having a wee cup of tea when a knock comes to the door.

She says, 'Jack, that'll be somebody for you again. I'm pestered sick with so many folk coming to the door – I wish you would stop making so many bellows!'

'Well, if I stop making bellows you'll no have so much to eat,' he says, 'or be so well off!'

So she said, 'I'll go and see who it is while you finish your tea.'

Out Jack's old mother goes to the door and she opens it. Standing in the door is an old, old woman with a big, long, spiky hat on her head.

She said, 'Is your son Jack in?'

'Aye,' she said.

'Is this where he sorts the bellows for blowing the fire?' the old woman said.

'Aye, he is in. What do you want of him?'

'I've got a set of bellows I want him to sort.'

'Well,' says Jack's mother, 'don't stand there, come on in! He's just having a wee mouthful of tea. Come on in, sit down a wee while and get a cup of tea.'

Now unknown to Jack and his old mother this was a witch, see! And she came from a place high up in the mountains called Blowaway Hill where the wind blew steadily day out and day in, where the wind was that strong you could hardly stand. And this old witch lived on Blowaway Hill where the wind always blew. In she comes. She sits down, and Jack's old mother gives her a wee cup of tea. And she opens this parcel she has with her and takes out a pair of bellows.

She says, 'Jack, I think you could sort those for me.'

'Aye,' he said, 'I could sort them.'

And Jack looked at them and he looked again. In all his days he had never seen a pair of bellows like these! They had a long, long brass point on the front, beautifully carved into the shape of a cat's head. And the two handles were two ducks' heads. They were made of solid brass. The leather in between them for gathering the air to blow the fire was completely finished. And Jack knew it was just the job for him, no bother at all!

She said, 'Do you think you could do anything with them?'

'Och,' he said, 'it's no bother to me to sort them.'

'But I'll tell you one thing,' she said: 'you'll have to be very, very careful because they belonged to my great-great-great-great-granny and I would like you to sort them and I'll make it worth your while.'

'All right,' says Jack. 'But where do you stay?'

'Have you ever heard of a place called Blowaway Hill?'

'I've heard my father speaking about it,' he said, 'it's a long road from here.'

'Well, I stay there. And if you sort the bellows and bring them up to me . . . I'm an old woman and I can't walk very far – it'll take me a long while to go home tonight – I'll have to be going home now, and thank your mother very much for the cup of tea . . . I'll make it worth your while.'

'Well, well, Granny,' he said, 'I'll bring them up to you when I'm finished.'

So the old woman went away. But she got around the corner – she looked round to see if anybody was watching – she jumped on her broomstick and off she goes through the sky! Home to Blowaway Hill! She landed at the door with her broomstick – into her own house and put the broomstick in at the back of the door.

Now Jack was left with his mother. Jack sat and took his tea.

'Mother,' he said, 'I've mended bellows many's the time and I even mended bellows for the king, as you know. And never in my day, even when my father used to have the workshop here, have ever I seen a set of bellows look like that! That is the bonniest set of bellows that ever I have seen in my life! I wish one thing,' he says, 'God that they were mine – I would never part with them!'

'Well,' said his mother, 'you'll have to sort them for the old woman, you can't keep them.'

'Oh no, I can't keep them! That's one thing I can't do,

I can't keep them. I'll sort them.' Because that was his trade.

So Jack takes them into his shop, loosens them down, cuts all the old rotten leather off the two sides of the bellows, picks out all the best wee nails he could get – all the lovely wee brass nails – cuts new leather, sets the bellows on, puts the new leather in them, puts the lovely wee nails in. And then he polished them. And he polished the brass. He polished the two ducks' heads and he polished the cat's head on the point (this was a big cat's head with its mouth open for the point of the bellows). And he fell in love with them when he saw them. He wished they were his own. 'I've never,' he said, 'seen bellows like that in my life!'

He was heart-sorry the next day when he had to roll them up in a wee parcel and take them back to Blowaway Hill, to the old witch's house on the mountain. Anyway, he got his breakfast and said good-bye to his mother.

And his mother said, 'What time will you be home – will you be home late tonight, Jack? It's a long road to Blowaway Hill to where the old woman stays. I've heard of her – folk says she's a witch!'

'Tsst! Ach, Mother,' he says, 'witch! You cry everybody a witch!'

'Well, I'll tell you one thing,' she said, 'she looks a civil enough old woman, but you never know about these old women, away on a hill staying in a big house away by herself up there. You never know what she's doing, working spells, one thing and another. I've heard many a bad story around the village about her.'

'Ah well, Mother, I'm away anyway, I'll see you tonight.'

Away goes Jack with the bellows in below his oxter, wrapped in a bit of soft, chamois leather. His mother gave him a bit piece* to take with him and he travels. He travels and he travels, oh, he travels a long, long time. He must have travelled for nearly half a day till he came to this wood, and a hill, and this path going up the hill right to the very top. A wee house was sitting on the top of the hill. And in the middle of the house was one chimney, and the wind was blowing on the chimney – the smoke around the chimney never went straight, it was always going zig-zag. Because there was always wind on the top of the hill where she stayed, they called it Blowaway Hill.

So Jack buckles his coat round about him, gets the bellows in below his oxter, and he walks up the narrow path till he arrives . . . 'God,' he says, 'it's cold here! How does this old woman, this old cratur of a woman, bide up here in that cold wind? It's no' half as cold down on the flat as it is up here.' But he knocked on the door and out came the old woman.

'Oh, it's you, son,' she said.

'Aye, it's me, Granny.'

'Come on in out of the cold wind!' she said. 'Ach, it's that North Wind – he's aye blowing in here. He never gives me peace. It's no' long since he's been in here getting his tea, a minute ago, and he'll be back here again. I'm fed up with him blowing into the house. I never get peace with him – the door rattling, the windows rattling and blowing my wee bits of sticks all over the place. I wish he would go away for a while and leave me at peace!'

'Who are you talking about?' said Jack.

She said, 'It's the North Wind I'm talking about.'

'But, Granny,' he said, 'the North Wind can't bother anybody.'

* bit piece – small sandwich

'Ah, but he bothers me, he comes in and bothers me,' she said, 'comes in here and sits down and gets his tea.'

Jack said to himself, 'I doubt she's a wee bit away with the birds,' he was thinking that when she took him in.

She said, 'Are you wanting something to eat?'

'Aye,' he said, 'I'll have something to eat,' and she made him a good tea.

But the windows started to rattle and shake and the house started to shake. And the wind blew down the chimney . . . the fire went out.

She says, 'Jack, did you get my bellows sorted?'

'Aye,' he says.

She says, 'Give me them!'

He gave them to her. She caught them. She set them down at the side of the fire and she said, 'Blow, bellows, blow!' And the bellows started to blow by themselves. They puffed and they blew and they puffed and they blew, and up, down, and up, and down and up and down and out and in and up and down and up and down and . . .

And Jack's sitting watching them – his two eyes are just sticking out of his head watching these bellows! The witch had put a spell on them: they were magic bellows! And he's watching – the fire kindled up in two minutes!

She said, 'Stop, bellows, stop!'

The bellows stopped – lay down. Jack's heart began to beat fast.

'Dear, dear,' he said to himself, 'if I had that! What could I do with that, I could travel all over the country and show off to folk . . . take it to the king! And I would be made for life,' he's thinking to himself, you see!

But anyway, the windows start to rattle and the door starts to blow and the wind comes down the chimney, 'Bvizzz!' the big heavy noise comes in. And in comes the

North Wind! He sits down in the chair. Jack has a look round about him.

'Who's that?' he says to the old witch.

'Ach, it's my friend,' she said, 'the cold North Wind. He's in for his tea.'

'Well,' he says, 'folk say you can see the wind but I never saw the wind before.'

'Well,' she said, 'you're seeing it now!'

The North Wind's sitting with this big long beard, long hair and a big long coat, and his feet stretched out – sitting in the chair. The old witch gave him a cup of tea sitting next to Jack in the chair.

So she told him, 'It's Jack from the village up sorting my bellows for me.'

The North Wind's sitting, (it could speak to the witch) and says, 'Oh aye,' he said, 'ah, those bellows I gave you years ago.'

She says, 'You never gave them to me years ago, North Wind. You gave them to my great-great-great-great-granny years ago.'

He said to her, 'But I see they're still working.'

'Aye, they're still working. Well anyway,' she said, 'Jack, it's getting late and the North Wind and I have got a lot of things to talk about. It's time you were getting away home.'

'Aye,' he said, 'I'll soon have to go home.'

'But wait a minute,' she says, 'I'll have to pay you, I'll have to pay you for sorting my bellows.' She says, 'What would you like?'

Jack's sitting and he thought a wee while. He said, 'There's only one thing I would like from my heart – a pair of bellows like those ones.'

'Ah, Jack, Jack!' she says. 'I couldn't give you those bellows . . . they're magic bellows. You just say, "Blow!" and they blow the fire themselves. And say "Stop!" and they stop themselves. But,' she says, 'if they ever get out of hand, if they get on their own, there's nothing but me can stop them.'

'Well,' he said, 'I don't care. I could do with a pair like that.'

'But wait a minute!' she says. 'I'll tell you what I'll do with you – I've an old set of bellows like that belonging to my auntie, my great-auntie, and they're needing sorted. If you could sort them . . .'

'But,' he says, 'I like the ducks on the handles and I like the cat . . .'

'They're the same thing, mounted the same way,' she said, 'but they're a wee bittie bigger.'

'That would do,' says Jack. 'If they're a wee bit bigger they'd be all the better.'

So, he took them. They were the same thing – looked the same but a wee bit different: instead of them being mounted with brass, they were common wood. But they had a long brass spout with a cat's head in the front and two ducks' heads for handles. The leather was finished inside them, but the rest was good. He looked at them, turned them all over.

'Aye,' he said, 'they're good enough bellows but they're not like yours – there's no magic in them.'

'Na, Jack, there's no magic in them,' she said, 'you'll have to blow the fire yourself with them.'

'But,' he said, 'could you no' give me a wee spell, just a wee toy kind of a spell, a bit of one? I'm not wanting very much magic in them . . . you being a witch – as folk say you're a witch and . . . you're bound to be a witch when you can speak to the North Wind and bring him into the house. I had a long walk up here, you know, and I had a big job sorting them.'

'Well, Jack, you make my heart run away with my head' she said, 'and as long as you look after them carefully, I'll put a wee spell on them for you and they'll blow themselves.'

'Good!' said Jack.

So she went in the back room, rumbled and rummaged with her hands, chanted words and things. She came out with the bellows in her hands.

'There you are, Jack,' she said.

'But wait a minute!' says the North Wind. 'Can you let me look at that wee spell before you give it to Jack – and I'll put it in the bellows for him?'

Ah, now the North Wind was wicked, you know. He wasn't bad – but he liked to play tricks on folk, see!

'I'll tell you what I'll do, seeing as I've met Jack here for the first time,' he said, 'let me put the spell into the bellows for him!'

'Well,' says the witch, 'I can't see any harm in that.'

So he caught the bellows from Jack, you see, and the North Wind said, 'I'll tell you what I'll do, I'll *blow* the spell in for you.' But in his own head he was thinking, 'I'll make it a wee bit stronger!' So he gave a hard blow into them and he says, 'We'll see the fun after this!' He put a *big* spell, a strong spell of wind, into the bellows. Poor Jack didn't know the difference!

Jack parcelled the bellows below his oxter, and he bade the witch good-bye and he bade the North Wind good-bye. He travelled away back home, oh, it was near midnight when he got home to the house! His old mother was waiting up for him. In he went. She gave him his supper.

She said, 'You weren't a while away!'

'No wonder, Mother, I was a while away!' he said. 'I had miles to walk and after I got there . . . you weren't far wrong – thon definitely was a witch.'

'Oh, as low as my father* she's a witch! She's a real witch.'

---

* as low as my father – as sure as the death of my father

'And to make things better, the North Wind was sitting in the house with her when I went up! Well, he wasn't there when I went up but he came in.'

'Tsst, laddie, have you been drinking?'

'Not me, Mother,' he said.

'What kind of drink did the witch give you?'

'The witch never gave me anything!'

'Well, she must have given you something,' she said, 'you're drunk – saying things like that.'

'No, Mother, I'm not drunk! I never had any drink of any kind.'

'North Wind!' she said. 'You know fine there's nobody can see the wind but a pig, a pig's the only one that can see the wind.' Well, they argued about it anyway.

'But, I'll tell you one thing, Mother,' he says: 'I got a lovely set of bellows for my job.'

'Is that all she gave you?' said the mother. 'She must have given you a sixpence or something.'

'No, she never gave me a ha'penny. I wasn't wanting any money – I got the bellows . . . and they're magic!'

'You and your magic!' she said. 'You're always looking for something magic.'

'Well, Mother, I've got it this time.'

But anyway, Jack took them down. And these bellows, when he'd sorted them up, he started to polish them, and he polished them and he polished them and he made them that bonnie that they were ten times bonnier than the other ones. The more he polished them the bonnier they got!

'Look,' he said, 'Mother, did you ever see the likes of *that* – those are the bonniest bellows in the world! Mother, they are fit for a king!'

'You're right, Jack, they are fit for a king,' she said. 'The best thing you can do now is go and take them to the king!'

'Oh, Mother, I couldn't.'

'Look,' she says, 'Jack . . .'

'Mother, I couldn't give my bellows to the king,' he said, 'they're magic.'

'Magic,' she says, 'there's no magic in them. If they're magic, prove it!'

'No, no,' he said, 'no, no, I'm no' wanting to prove it, no no. They're magic for me.'

But the old mother got him coaxed and she looked at him. 'Jack, they are bonnie bellows right enough. They're the bonniest bellows that ever I've seen. Look at the cat's head in the front and look at those ducks' heads on the handles! Your father,' she said, 'God rest him, made hundreds of bellows and sorted many's the set in this shop years before – and your grandfather before him. But, never in my days have I seen a set of bellows like that! They are fit for a king! Jack, son, the best thing you can do is go to the royal gate, to the palace and hand them into the king. And I bet any money,' she said, 'you'll get a good price for them.'

But they argued. He wasn't wanting to sell them, but anyway she got him talked into it.

So the next day Jack packed the bellows below his oxter in a bit of skin and he set sail for the king's palace to show the king his bellows, see? So he travelled on and travelled, he hadn't very far to go, through the village and away out to the end of the village and there was the king's big palace and all the lovely big gardens round about. And he walked up the path leading up to the garden. At the same time who was in the garden but the queen! And she was cutting roses in the garden.

Jack came walking up . . . now he has these bellows wapped in a bit of leather, bonnie soft skin. He walks up the pad.

'Oh!' the queen said. 'Good – bonnie young man, are you the gardener?'

'No, no,' he said, 'I'm not the gardener; I want to see the king.'

'Well, I'll tell you what to do,' she said, 'he's sitting in the castle just now, the palace, and if you follow me, I'll lead you to him.' The queen was very nice to him. But she went to step out in front of Jack and she had a bunch of roses, flowers that she'd cut – and they fell on the ground.

And Jack, being a good lad, said, 'Wait, Your Majesty, and I'll lift the flowers!' He bent down to lift the flowers for the queen and didn't the bellows fall out of his oxter onto the ground!

'Oh, what a lovely set of bellows!' said the queen. 'It's the very thing I want, they're the very thing I want to blow my fire. I've always wanted a set of bellows in my bedroom to blow my fire, and I'll give you anything for them!'

'Well,' says Jack, 'I was hoping to take them, to show them to the king,' but he didn't tell her they were magic bellows!

So the queen couldn't wait till she got these bellows and she's admiring them. She says to Jack, 'You carry the flowers, and I'll carry the bellows!' In she goes to her bedroom.

Now Jack said to her, 'Look, there's a wee spell on those, on those bellows, and they work themselves. You don't need to pump them with your hands.'

'Oh, that's better,' she said. 'I'm delighted! I'll have to shout for His Majesty the King and shout for everybody in the castle to have them come and see these magic bellows. You'll get anything you want for them.'

So the queen caught her flowers and she stuck them into nice vases round about the room. She shouted for the king, the cook, the footman, the butler, for everybody to come in and see these magic bellows. And the fire, they had a great big fire. (Oh, the old-fashioned fires in the big castles were great big monster fires. And it was all sticks, they had no coal to burn in those days.)

She said, 'How do they work?'

'Well, you just put them down at the fire and you say, "Blow, bellows, blow!"'

And the big, old, fat king – oh, he's dying to see this, you see! And the cook comes in, the butler comes in, the footman comes in, and the queen – she's standing close to the bellows.

She said, 'Blow, bellows, blow!'

And the bellows started to blow, and they blew the fire clean up the chimney. And they started to blow – now, the North Wind had put a *big* spell in them, you see – and they blew the queen's hair right out straight, all that bonnie lovely yellow hair, blew the queen's hair all the way back. They blew the roses out of the vases. They blew the king up and he stuck to the chandeliers. And the bellows started to go around the room and around the room, and they blew on the footman; they blew up the clothes of the cook and she was battering them with a stew pot and she couldn't stop them!

They go out through the door and round the castle, round the palace, and are blowing all the flowers down, blowing the trees down . . . the king, he's shouting for somebody to come and help, for the footman to go and get a ladder to get him down. And the cook's after these bellows with a skillet, she's trying to skelp the bellows – but no, she can't stop them. Now poor Jack didn't know what to do, he's dumbfounded.

He's shouting, 'Stop, bellows!' No! The more he shouted the worse it got.

The queen's shouting for the bellows to stop, the whole castle is in an uproar with these bellows. They're blowing everything in the castle outside in, but no, they can't stop them!

Jack says, 'There's nothing for it! I'll never get them stopped in the world – there's only one cure, I'll have to go back for the witch – no other cure!'

So it's off with his two boots. Jack rolled up his trousers and he set sail back, and he ran and he ran and he ran.

Now all this time he was away these bellows were still going, round the castle and round the castle and they blew every stick of furniture, everything, out of the castle. They blew all the trees down at the castle, blew everything out of the garden, these bellows. And they're going round in circles, puffing and blowing wherever they could get. Nobody could stop them. And the king! He's hiding away into a cupboard and he's got a hold of the queen with the fright of this thing, with the wind in these bellows. And he's shouting for Jack, but Jack's gone. So Jack ran and he ran and he ran as fast as he could. He was out of breath as he ran to the top of the hill.

And he told the witch, 'Oh . . .'

'What is it, Jack?' she said. 'Lord, what's wrong with you, laddie?'

'Look,' he says, 'I ran all the way . . .' and he told her the story. 'I went to the . . .'

'Oh, you did the wrong thing,' she said. 'But I put a spell in the bellows – I only gave it a spell to kindle your fire and no more . . . aye, Jack, I know who it was – it was the North Wind up to his tricks again! It was him, he blew into it and he made those bellows like that. God knows what'll happen now,' she said, 'with the disturbance it caused down at the palace, Jack!'

'I'm in trouble,' he said, 'because it was me who went with the bellows in the first place. I'll probably get my head cut off, the king will maybe put me to the dungeon!'

'No, I'll tell you what to do: you run away back and I'll be there as quickly as you. And I'll put a stop to the bellows,' says the old witch. 'See!'

She went out the back door, jumped on her broomstick, got the broomstick between her legs and away she went, *whist!* through the air, and she landed in front of the castle just in minutes.

Here the bellows are still going – they're puffing and blowing around the castle and blowing the dust around, blowing in the windows. They had blown the queen's feather-bed till there was nothing left, they'd scattered the feathers all over the palace for miles. They'd blown every stitch of clothes off the cook and she's standing shivering at the back of the door. And the butler – he's worse!

Anyway, the witch landed – right in front of the bellows. And the bellows are circling, puffing and blowing and puffing round in circles.

So the witch stops and she draws a big circle and she points to the bellows. 'Come here! Come you to me, bellows!' And the bellows stopped blowing. And they came round, came round and came back – when they came right into the middle of the circle the witch made a snap at them – and their power was gone. She pumped the bellows, pumped them, two-three times – no more wind. 'Right!' she said.

So everything quietened down at the castle and she went up to the king, 'Look, Your Majesty, it wasn't Jack . . .' And she told the king the story that I'm telling you. She said, 'It was the North Wind; Jack had nothing to do with it.'

'Well!' says the king. 'It'll take weeks, maybe months to put this castle back the way it was, but somebody has to pay for it.'

'Well,' says the witch, 'it wasn't Jack.'

'He was the one who came,' said the king.

'I'll tell you what I'll do,' she said; 'it was the North Wind that caused all the trouble, and I'll send him to you and you can make him pay for what he did.'

So Jack went into the king and the king forgave Jack. And the queen looked at the bellows – oh, she was terrified!

The witch says, 'No, no, Your Majesty the Queen, you're all right.' In one spell the witch put everything back to normal, everything back the way it had been.

'Everything's back to normal,' the king said, 'but somebody has to suffer for what I suffered with those bellows.' When the queen saw the bellows, she liked them but she was afraid to touch them.

'Go on!' said the witch. 'Go up to them, catch them, blow the fire with them!'

And the queen was kind of frightened, you know. She went up, she caught the bellows and she puff-puff-puff-puffed the fire. The fire blazed up beautifully . . . and the queen fell in love with the bellows. And she gave Jack a big bag of gold for the bellows and everybody was contented.

'But no,' said the king, 'there's one man who's got to come yet and be reckoned with. And that's the North Wind.'

'Well,' says the witch, 'I'll send him to you when I go back.'

So the witch jumped on her broomstick and back she went to Blowaway Hill where her house was. And sitting on Blowaway Hill in her wee house was the North Wind.

And he's sitting and he's laughing, 'Ho-ho-ho-ho-ho!' Oh, he's laughing away to himself. He could see what was going on, you see!

'Aye,' said the witch, 'it was nothing to laugh about. You nearly got poor Jack in a lot of trouble with your carry on.'

'Well, I didn't mean any harm, it was only for fun,' he said. 'I blew into the bellows and made the spell a wee bit stronger.'

'You nearly got Jack hanged. And if I hadn't got there in time and settled things,' she said, 'God knows what would have happened to the poor laddie! But anyway, all's well that ends well.'

'Ah well,' he said, 'that's it.'

'No, that's not it!' says the witch. 'You're wanted back at the palace – the king wants you!'

'What does he want me for?' asked the North Wind.

'He wants you for what you did!'

'Well, there hasn't been any wind around the palace for a long while . . . I'll have to go when His Majesty calls on me,' said the North Wind – 'I'll have to go!'

The king was lying back in his palace, he and the queen, when all in a minute the wind started round and round the castle, 'Whooo, whooo,' in through the window – right to the king's feet.

'Who are you?' said the king.

'I'm the North Wind.'

'Oh you are?' says the king. 'You're the North Wind, eh? You're the man that caused all the trouble with the bellows?'

'I am,' said the North Wind, 'and I've come to beg your pardon.'

'Well, look,' the king explained, 'I'm not in a bad mood now; but I was in a bad mood for a while and, you know, I'm not a bad king.'

'Well, I'm thankful for that!' says the North Wind.

'But one thing you'll have to do for me,' he said. 'I'm going to let you off on one condition: when there comes bonnie, warm warm days at my palace; when there's not a breath of wind, round my palace, and everything is warm and hot and there's not a breeze to be seen, and the trees and everything are quiet; I want *you* to come and blow a cold breeze about me whenever I get hot.'

'Right!' said the North Wind.

So he and the king shook hands on it, and he bade the king farewell. And after that, the king had never any need to worry! Because when it was hot blazing sun and there wasn't a cloud in the sky, the king could lie back and enjoy a cool, cool breeze from the North Wind.

And the witch was happy and Jack was happy and that's the last of my wee story.

This was a story I heard from an old uncle of mine who used to come to Argyll . . . he's dead now, God rest his soul . . . I was only four years old and I walked down to see him one summer's evening. And he told me and my cousins so many stories that it was too late for me to go home so I stayed the whole night with him till the morning and he told us stories all night. His name was Alexander Reid, he died about four years ago and he's buried in Helensburgh.

Jack and his Mother's Cloth

Now I want to tell you a story . . . It's about Jack and his old mother. They stayed in this wee croft, and for a while he worked away with his old mother in this place. Och, and things got kind of bad with the old wife. She had a cow, it supplied them with a wee drop of milk. But anyway it went dry. The tatties weren't growing and they had no hay or anything; they had spent every shilling she had.

So one day she said to Jack, 'Jack, there's nothing for it. You're no looking for a job. You're lying about the house now doing nothing. You're not like your old father, God rest him; he worked all the days of his life to bring you up to be a man as you are. But now, you never do anything, you never go to the town . . . and me, I can't afford to keep you! My cow's dry, the hens aren't laying, there's no eggs or devil a haet*. And look at the state of me – I'm just about naked, there's not a stitch of clothes on my back with scrimping and scriving and saving to rear you up to what you are today. And what do you do for me? Nothing! The best thing you can do in the morning when you see God's daylight, is to take the old cow in to the market and sell it! And that'll be the end of the lot. If you don't get a job to yourself . . . well,

* devil a haet – nothing at all

it's up to you, you're not going to survive. For the rest of my days, for all the years I've got left, I'm no caring what happens to me. It's up to yourself.'

'Well, Mother,' he said, 'if it makes you happy, the morn* I'll go into the town and I'll sell your old cow, it's getting kind of groany.'

'Aye,' she says, 'it's getting kind of old but it was all we had! Anyway, it'll no matter. But I'll tell you: if you sell it, would you get me a wee bit of cloth for to try and make a few clothes for myself? You see the state of the rags I'm in. Buy me a roll of cloth! It'll no cost you very much. And I'll make myself some kind of a frock, or blouse, or a skirt or something. I can't afford to buy any.'

'All right,' says Jack.

He gets up in the morning, has a wee bit breakfast, gets the old cow with a halter and away he goes to the town with it – walking, pulling it behind him. Into the market and he wanders around . . . Oh, the farmers were in with nice beasts and everybody's here – it was the market day!

Anyway, with all the prigging and preaching† round about the town Jack met this dealer who bought old beasts like his. All the money he could get for it was six guineas. He sold it.

So he said to himself, 'My mother told me to get two-three messages‡ and get the wee bit cloth for her to make a frock for herself.'

Oh, but true to his word, he went into the shop and he bought a roll of the nicest, fanciest cloth he could get for his old mother! He went into the shop and got messages, butter

---

* the morn – tomorrow
† prigging and preaching – fine talk to persuade people to buy
‡ two-three messages – a few groceries

and sugar and tea and everything his mother needed, and packed them in a box. He had four guineas left.

'Well,' he says, 'Mother's cow here or Mother's cow there, I'm going to have a wee drink to myself before I go home.'

In he goes to the hotel. He sits down and he's cracking away to the old men. And he's drinking, he's drinking and he's drinking . . . he looks at his money. He had one guinea left.

'Ah well, that's it,' he said, 'that's it! Ach, I can't help it,' he says to the barman, 'Give me a half-bottle of whisky!'

He shoves it in his pocket; he looks at his money again – two five-shilling pieces he had left. He drinks that. Now he's well on. It's closing time, ten o'clock, getting dark. He lifts his web of cloth below his oxter and his box of messages in his hand, his half-bottle's in his pocket and he's away wandering back the road, travelling back speaking away to himself and singing – oh, he's in a good, happy state.

He said, 'I have no money for Mother. I don't know what I'm going to do for the morn. I've spent the lot.' He didn't mean to spend it, but he spent the lot of it.

But on his way back he had to go through this wood, you see. And in this wood there were a lot of thorn trees and hedges. He came to this wee tree. It was only a low thorn tree but it was two wee twin trees growing together, growing close together. He was drunk. And it was a heavy night's wind.

The tree was blowing with the wind back and forward and going, 'Squeak, squeak, squeak!'

He stops, well on with drink, oh, he's just about passing out. 'By God!' he said to himself, 'what is an old cratur of a woman like you doing here this night?'

'Old Woman,' he said, 'what are you doing out in a night like this!'

'Squeak, squeak, squeak,' went the bush.

'Can you no come home with me to my old mother and get shelter for the night, and get a lie down, instead of sitting there this time of night among that cold wind? I bet you a guinea it's going to be rain tonight – you'll be soaked to the skin. Come on, old wife! Come home with me!'

The tree went, 'Squeak, squeak, squeak.' No move.

'Ah well,' he said, 'I can't carry you if you'll no come, I can't coax you any longer. My old mother will be getting worried about me, but you're welcome to come home with me if you want to. You'll definitely die with the cold if you stay there more the night, you'll definitely die, old wife! Ach, the hell with it!' Rolls out the web of cloth – his mother's cloth to make his mother's clothes – and he waps it round the wee tree, round and round and round the tree. 'That'll keep you warm, old wife,' he said, 'till tomorrow. I'll aye come back in the morning and get it if you're still living.' Lifts his box with his messages and away he goes wandering home.

His old mother's sitting with a good fire on. 'Is that you back, laddie?'

'Aye, I'm back, Mother.'

'How did you get on?'

'Well, Mother, to tell you the God's truth, I never got on very well.'

She says, 'What did you get for the old cow?'

He said, 'I got six guineas for it.'

'Did you get anything to eat, did you get me a smoke?' The old woman smoked a pipe.

'Aye, Mother, I got you tobacco. And there's tea and sugar and plenty of butter and cheese and all the messages and there's a wee half-bottle for you – drink it before you go to your bed!'

'Na, I'll no drink it myself,' she says, 'I'll give you half of it. Sit down there!'

She sat down and the two of them shared the half-bottle between them. Now she's well on, the old wife, after this. (She drank most of the half-bottle, you see!)

'By the way, Jack, did you get my wee bit cloth to make me some kind of a skirt, a frock or something to go on me?'

'Aye, Mother, I got you a lovely bit cloth.'

'Ach, well, I'll get it in the morning from you.'

'No, Mother,' he said, 'you'll no get it in the morning.'

She says, 'What do you mean – I'll no get it in the morning?'

'Well, you know the path – as you're coming up the pad from the town?'

'Aye, I know it well. Many's the time me and your father walked it.'

'Well,' he said, 'on the road* sitting on the side of the path was an old woman. And I think, Mother, she was deaf because I roared to her and roared to her and she wasn't hearing me. And the cold wind . . . I got sorry for her. And I took your wee bit o' cloth and I wrapped it round her to keep her warm. I'll go back for it for you in the morning.'

'Ah well,' she said (being well on with drink), 'you're a good-hearted laddie, Jack. I would like somebody to do that for me if I was sitting like that at night among the cold wind. Why didn't you bring her back with you?'

'Mother, she wouldn't come – I coaxed her like a lamb of God – she wouldn't come. But I'll go back for your wee bit of cloth in the morning.'

'All right, Jack,' she said, 'I'm away to my bed.' The old woman went away to her bed. He went away to his.

But true to his word, Jack's up at six o'clock in the morning getting clear†; makes himself a cup of tea, and whistling away down the road goes back for his mother's cloth.

* on the road – along the way
† getting clear – break of day

Now you can imagine if you wap thin silk cloth around a thorn tree during a heavy night's wind and gale, what was going to happen to it: it flapped and it tore and it flipped and it fleeped all fairin night. It was torn in ribbons from bit to bit. There was not a yard that was whole but it was torn to holes with the jaggy tree! He looked at the tree.

'It was you!' he said. 'Tree! A wee bush. Did I no think – me with the drink on me – you were an old woman! And that's the thanks you give me – tore my mother's wee bit cloth . . . you must have been a witch. You were a witch and you picked that tree, you changed into a tree! But I'll give you a tree and all you want – I'm going back for a spade and I'm going to dig you out and you'll never, never bother another body coming up this pad!'

Back he goes to his mother's shed and takes out a spade. Away with it on his shoulder, down he goes. And he digs round the tree – true to his word, he digs right round the tree, cuts every root and gives the tree a pull out by the root and flings it about ten feet away from him.

'There,' he said, 'bush, you'll no aggravate me anymore!'

But he looked where he pulled the tree out; there was a hole. And he keeked down. He says, 'What's that down there?'

He scrapes back the sand with his two hands – an iron box in below the three. Padlock on it. Lifts it out, breaks the padlock with his spade . . . it was full of gold sovereigns to the mouth, about two thousand sovereigns in this box, in below the tree! Well, he went down on his knees – he didn't know what to do, he didn't know what to do he was so glad! He put the box on his back and he ran back to his mother. He told her.

She said, 'Jack, Jack, laddie! We're made for life, don't tell a soul! This'll do me and you for the rest of our days. That must have been hidden for years in below that tree.'

'Mother,' he said, 'it's all right for you but what about the wee tree? But for it we wouldn't have any money tonight. Give me a pail of water!' He filled a pail of water.

With it and the spade back he goes. He lifts the wee tree carefully as he could, stretches every wee root on it, puts it back in the hole, covers it with sand and spreads all the water round – gives it a good drink.

'Now,' he says, 'I'll come back every day and give you a pail of water till you start to grow again.'

And he went back every day and fed that wee tree till it started to grow again. The next year it was blossoming – full in bloom. And he and his old mother lived happily with the money they got below the tree ever after.

And that's the last of the wee story!

I heard a couple of different versions of this one – from my Uncle Duncan Townsley in Kintyre, Johnnie MacDonald from Perthshire and old Johnnie Townsley from Campbeltown.

The Boy and the Boots

The Travellers believed that there were people who lived in this world long before your time and mine who used to steal people away and take their bodies, kill them and cut them up, and use them for research in colleges for the education of doctors. The tinkers and Travellers called them 'burkers' – body-snatchers. And they still believe that there are plenty of body-snatchers alive at this present moment, though the demand for bodies is no' as much as it was in the olden days.

We used to say to our daddy, 'Daddy, tell us a wee story when you were near burkit with the body-snatchers.'

Daddy turned around and said, 'Well, I'll tell you a wee burker story that happened to me a long time ago when I was very young.

'Me and my mother and father and the rest of the children were in this town. We had travelled all over the country and we were in a new town every day, and this was a strange town to us because we had never been here before. I was about fourteen at the time. We landed in the town and my mother was selling some baskets, my daddy was making and selling some tin. We always used to go and sit on the village green. My daddy would maybe go and have a wee drink and my mother would make us some tea. We could play ourselves in the village green but we didn't interfere with the rest of the children that inhabited the village; we kept to ourselves.

'But I got very curious, because I had never got much room to be on my own for a wee while. I said to myself I would have a wander through the town, see all the beautiful things that I had never seen. Because naturally, Travelling people like us never had much chance to come to the town unless it was the weekend, when my daddy had something to sell.

'So I wandered through the town – there were shops full of clothing, beautiful clothes that I would love to own but had no way of getting; and there were shops full of toys and shops full of food, butcher shops full of meat – it just made my mouth water! And I passed my time in the town for a long long while. But time had passed so fast for me I never realized that, looking at all these things in the town, hours had passed, and I had to go back. I made my way to the green where my mummy and daddy were supposed to be waiting for me. But when I landed back my mummy and daddy were gone! They had packed their little handcart with the tent – they went and left me.

'I'm left in the middle of the town, and I never knew in a million years what direction my father went! He could have gone south, he could have gone east, he could have gone west, he could have gone in any direction. So I said to myself, "Now, I'll have to find my mother and father," because I was only fourteen and I'd never been left by myself before and I'd never spent a night away from my father and mother in my life. And my father had told me all the stories about evil people who were burkers with coaches who would take my body and sell it to the doctors for money – I was terrified.

'But anyway, I thought I'd take the main road out of the

village because I thought that's the road my mummy and daddy would take. And I travelled on and travelled on, and by the time I got to the end of the town it was getting dark. And I said to myself, "I'll never catch my mummy and daddy tonight, what am I going to do? I can't stay by myself," because I was afraid.

'So I travelled on and I travelled on and I travelled on, and the farther I travelled the darker it got, because it was the winter months and it got darker by the minute. It was very very dark when I came to a long straight piece of road between two forests with not a house in sight.

'Then I listened! And I heard coming behind me – the patter of horses' feet. The thought dawned in my head, the stories my daddy had told me – the burkers' coach! I said, "This is bound to be a burkers' coach!"

'And I got in the ditch among the long grass, I hid down in the ditch. Then I heard the horses' coach coming, the patter of horses' feet – they passed me by. There were two horses on the coach and the coach was all in black except for one light on the roof. I waited and waited and waited, till the coach got well on before me.

'I said to myself, "As sure as God in heaven, my daddy told me, that is a burkers' coach out looking for bodies tonight. Well, they're not going to get me!"

'So I travelled on, I travelled on, I travelled on, and I came to this piece of road going up a wee piece of hill, and lying in the road was a pair of boots – the most beautiful boots I had ever seen in my life – long brown leather boots! And they were tied together with a pair of laces. I picked up the boots and said, "This'll do me," because I wanted – all my life – I had wanted to own a pair of boots like this. And I put them across my shoulder.

'I travelled on for about ten yards. And I looked – there

was a gate. The moon began to come up. I looked in the gate and I saw all these things standing up, all these white things standing up. But I wasn't afraid! Out again – the moon got brighter – and I saw that it was a graveyard, and the gates were open. Now my daddy had always told me, "You're safe enough passing a graveyard if you don't pass it by between twelve and one." I knew that I had left the village when it was only getting dark, that now it could only be about nine or ten o'clock. It couldn't be *evil* time in the graveyard. So I naturally walked past the gates of the graveyard, about ten yards from where I had found the boots – they were on my back.

'I travelled on, I travelled on, this long weary road. I looked at all the places at the roadside to see if I could see a light of a campfire or something – but no, there was no light or campfire.

'But now the hoolits began, "cahoo-cahoo-cahoo". It was night-time, the road was long and dreary – I got kind of afraid. I said, "I just can't stay tonight, out, I can't sleep under a hedge or something," because I had never done it before. And I travelled on, there wasn't a house in sight.

'Then, above the road a wee bit, I saw a light. And this road led up to it. Now my daddy had always said to me, "If you're down and out, look for a light well back from the road because coaches and burkers didn't go off the road – it was too much of a pull for the horses."

'So I see this light up on a hillside and there was an old rough road going up the way. I said, "Probably it's an old farmer and his wife, probably I can sleep in the shed for the night and nobody'll know I'm there till the morning. And I'll jump out and be gone before they ever see me."

'So I walked up, slowly up the road, but my feet were making terrible noises on the coarse stones going up it. I walked up and walked up and walked up; I just landed at the end of the road when out comes a man with a lantern. He had one of these old-fashioned lights in his hand, a paraffin lamp. And he sees me before I had a chance to get into the shed and lie down – he sees me.

'He says, "Come here, you!"

'So naturally I was a wee bit afraid, and he came forward. He held the light up and shined it in my face – he looked at me.

'"And – hey," he said, "who are you and where do you come from?"

'"Oh," I said, "Sir, I'm sorry – I must have taken the wrong road. I'm looking for my daddy and my mummy and the children, my wee brothers and sisters."

'He said, "Say that again?"

'I said, "I'm looking for my mummy and my daddy and my wee brothers and sisters."

'He said, "Who are you?" And he shined the light on me, saw I was ragged and torn and my clothes weren't very . . . "Are you one of the tinker people?"

'"Oh," I said, "yes, sir, I'm one of the tinker people – I'm the oldest of the family and I was in the town today back there with my mummy and daddy and I lost them and I didn't know what road to take. And I, I-I'm looking for them."

'He said, "Come with me."

'He took me past the house right to the door, opened the door of the big shed, a barn. He said, "Get in there! You can sleep in there for the night, you'll be all right!" He closed the door and he locked it. I heard the key going "click".

'I walked forward through the barn and it was heaped with straw. And then I looked – there was a stall in the one corner, in the stall was a cow and the cow was chewing hay. I looked up, there were some couples up above the cow's head and on the roof there was a sky-light – I could see the moon shining through it. I tried the door but the door wouldn't open; there was no other way out.

'I said to myself, "I don't like this very much. I can't stay here. I don't like this man very much."

'But anyway, I sat down among some straw and then I heard the key turning in the door. The door opened. And the light shone on me.

'He said, "Are you there?"

'I said, "Yes, I'm here – what is it?"

'"Come awa, come out a minute!"

'I came out. And this man who had the lantern was about six feet tall, *red-haired, with brown eyes*, a red face.

'He said, "Eh, I suppose you'll be hungry?"

'"Well, sir," I said, "I've had nothing to eat all day."

'"Well," he said, "come with me!"

'And he led me into the house. In the house was a big old-fashioned fire and a bare table, nothing on the table, some chairs. And there was this woman, about the same size as the man, with *red hair*, freckles on her face. And I looked at the other side of the table – there was a young man who must have been his son, and sitting on the other chair was his daughter – she was *red-haired*! And my daddy had told me, "Beware of red-headed people, especially farmers or land-owners who are red-haired and have brown eyes!" He told me they were bad people. "Never be sure of red-haired people or brown-eyed folk, keep away from them." And me – I was as blonde as a baby, fair curls down the back of my neck and blue eyes.

'And the farmer's wife said, "Isn't he a pretty little boy – it's a pity . . ."

'When she said, "it's a pity", didn't I think it was a pity that I had lost my daddy and my mummy! I didn't know!

'She said, "Isn't it a pity, isn't he a beautiful boy! Where do these Travelling tinker people get all the good looks and the beautiful hair and blue eyes?"

'But I didn't pay much attention. I heard her saying this but it didn't dawn on me then what she was meaning.

'She said, "Are you hungry?"

'I said, "Yes, ma'am, I'm hungry." So she brought me a big bowl of porridge and milk.

'She said, "Eat that up!" So I sat there and I was really hungry and I ate this big bowl of porridge and milk.

'Then the man took the lantern and he said, "You sure you're all right now – had you enough to eat?"

'I didn't like him very much because he had a big high Roman nose, hooked nose, curly red hair and evil-looking brown eyes.

'"Come on," he said, "I'll take you to your bed!" And he took me back into the same place. "You can find a place to sleep among the straw." And the cow was busy chewing away on the hay, chewing away.

'So I lay down but I couldn't sleep among the straw, I couldn't sleep. I said to myself, "I remember all the things that my daddy and mummy told me about red-haired people – they swore that they were burkers!" And they had a reason to believe that, because they had known from past experience these people really would sell someone's body for money. And I was terrified.

'Now I had left my boots in the shed when the farmer took me in to give me some supper. And I picked my boots up, put them around my neck, and I said, "I'll have to find a way to escape." But the door was locked – I couldn't escape, there was no way out. "I'll have to escape!" And then the moon came up again, it shined through the skylight and I said to myself, "That's the way out for me!"

'Me being a tinker, I knew how to get out. I said, "I'll climb up that wall and I'll get through that skylight window." But the thing was, the skylight was directly above the cow and the cow was tied right at the bottom. The cow wouldn't bother me. Now there were two long wooden beams to the left of the cow's head that went straight up to the roof. I said, "I'll climb that beam and get up there, open that window, go out on the roof and escape – get going! But," I said again, "probably I'm just exaggerating a wee bit. Probably if I stay here the people'll not bother me."

'Then I lay for a wee while, not asleep, when I heard a horse and coach coming in to the front of the farm, with lights on it. It stopped!

'And the farmer came out with a lamp in his hand and he said, "Okay! Come in and have a wee drink! I've got something for you tonight, I have something for you."

'And the man who stepped down from the coach had this long coat on him, a swallow-tail coat and a tile hat*. Three of them stepped from the coach, three men. And I could see by the light – with their long coats and their hats, they were the evil people my father had told me about. I could see the horse, a black horse, and a black coach parked right in front of the farm.

'I said to myself, "They're here for me! But they're no going to get me!"

'"Come in and have a drink," he said, "you can pick him up later!" That was *me* they were talking about – they were going to pick me up later! They were going to burk me, take me and kill me and sell my body to the doctors.

'I said, "No-o-o-o, they're no going to get me!"

'So I picked the boots up, put them around my neck and started to climb the pole above the cow's head – right to the

* tile hat – high, square-topped hat

sky-light. And I climbed and I climbed. I got up and I put my arms right up, and as I reached up my arms the boots fell off my neck. But as the boots fell, I looked – ooh, I nearly fell off too – there were legs in the boots cut from below the knee! Raw bloody legs, and they fell right at the cow's nose! I managed to reach the sky-light window and lifted it – it was open. I lifted it up slowly, crawled out through the hole, got out on the roof, ran along the roof. And I looked all around, it was kind of dark, and I jumped.

'I said, "I'm no caring suppose I break both my legs, I'll crawl on the grass before I get taken with these people."

'And then I landed – in the dung heap in the back of the place. It was lucky for me that the farmer had packed all the dung at the back of the shed. I landed right to the waist in the heap; I never even hurt a bone in my body. And I crawled out and ran away for my life, down through the moor and on to the main road. I said, "I'll make my way back to the town as fast as I can!" Now I don't know what happened behind me, but this is what I believe happened.

'After they had something to drink, the farmer said to the three men, "I've something for you tonight, a nice young man for you. I've got him locked up in the byre with the cow. And he's a good specimen. You can have him tonight!" And they paid the farmer a lot of money – for *me*, for my body! The farmer said, "He can't escape – I've got him locked up. Just grab him when you go in!"

'They opened the door and they looked all around with their lights. But they couldn't find me – I was gone! They searched every place in the byre. They couldn't get me.

'And then somebody said, "Maybe he's hiding behind the cow." They took a light up beside the cow and the cow was chewing away at the grass.

'"Maybe he's hiding under the cow's head, at the front of it." And they looked – "Oh!" somebody said. "Oh look, there's his boots – grab him!" And they grabbed the boots and they pulled them out and looked . . . nothing in the boots but the legs.

'The farmer said, "That's him, that's his boots – I remember his boots." (He'd never noticed, the boots had been on my back.) He said, "I never knew – a cow ate him, the cow has eaten him!"

'And the poor simple cow was standing chewing away at its cud. It had saved my life – chewing away, chewing its cud. And they believed the cow had eaten me! Because the boots that I had found at the gate of the graveyard had legs in them, and they believed that was me.

'And I made my way back the next morning. I hid in the wood till the sun came up, then made my way back to the town. I wandered round the town and the first body I found was my mother, who was in tears looking for me.

'She said, "Where have you been?"

'"Oh, Mother, where have you been, where have I been? Look, Mummy . . ." and I started to cry. I said, "I can't tell ye the noo* but I'll tell you the night when you take – take me home to my daddy!"

'She said, "I'm in here looking for you – your daddy's only along the shore a wee bit. We've got our camp just at the end of the town. I'm only in for to get some messages to make something for the bairns to eat. We're frantic looking for you all night. We're near off our heads looking for you!"

'I said, "Mummy, take me back." So my mummy took me back.

* the noo – right now

'My daddy said, "Where have you been?"

'"Daddy, listen, and I'll tell you where I've been . . ." and I told my daddy the story that I told you.

'And that is the God's honest truth – that really happened. That was me when I was near burkit many many years ago!'

This was our favourite story that Daddy used to tell us; it was one of his favourites too – he told it to us as children often.

The Pot that went to the Laird's Castle

This old Traveller man and his wife had three weans and they came to this place late one afternoon. It was about the back-end of the year and the man had made two-three baskets. He and the wife had a wee pram, a wee handcart. And they came up this glen they had never been before, up this long road going to an estate.

And he said to her, 'Look, you'll have to try and get something for the wee weans mair the night because it's getting kind of late. Give these baskets for anything at all, anything to make a bite to them for the night.'

The old woman said, 'This is a bad place we've come to, Johnnie, a bad place. I've called every house and every farm off and on the road and I cannae get a haet, not a thing.'

And the three wee weans were sitting on top of the barra and they're dying with hunger. But anyway, they travelled up this glen and at last they came to a waste farm at the roadside.

'Well,' she said, 'this is the last farm.'

'Well, I don't know what I'm doing up here,' he said, 'in the name of God.'

'Well,' she said, 'it's about three hundred yards from this backroad to the farm. Wait there and I'll go up and I'll ask the woman, I'll give her these two baskets. I'll try my best, see if I can get the makings of a wee taste of tea and sugar, anything at all to the weans for the night.'

So the man said, 'All right. And if you see the old gadgie or an old shepherd, ask him for a wee bit tobacco to me. An old shepherd of any kind.'

So the woman walked up the road to this farm and when she landed up it was the clartiest farm she'd ever seen in her life – the hens were scraping around the place, pigs were running about, the doorstep had never been swept for months. The door was lying open – she heard this body singing. She knocked at the door canny, she was afraid to knock in case the woman would put her away. But she knocked and this woman came out, a woman about seventeen stone, fat, with a sheet apron on her and a mutch on her head. She came out and she was smiling, brother!

'Hello, my dear,' she said, 'where did you come from?'

'Oh, I came up the glen,' she said, 'up this glen.'

'What is it you want? It's no many times we see people up here.'

'Well, to tell you the truth, I'm one of the Travelling folk, and I'm just wondering if you were needing any baskets?'

'Did you say "baskets"?'

'Aye, I was wondering, were you needing any baskets?'

'Oh, baskets!' she said. 'I've been trying to get a basket for years, and I can't get one. What are you wanting for your baskets? How much money are you wanting for them?'

She said, 'I'm no wanting any money for them. My man is sitting down at the road end there and my three wee weans are starving with hunger – I wonder if you would give me the makings of a wee cup of tea for the night for them?'

'Give you something? Come in – come in a minute, come in to the kitchen.' This woman took her in. She said, 'My man's away on the hill, he'll no be back for hours. You look kind of fabbat and kind of weak, woman! Wait a minute!'

And she went to the dresser, she took out a bottle of

brandy. She filled a glass, said, 'Drink that!' Full glass of brandy! She took one herself. 'And sit down there and tell me your story.'

So the story, this is the way it went: 'Well, me and my man, we came up this place, we'd never been here before, and we were going up the glen to see if this road would take us out to some other road.'

The farm woman said to her, 'Look, my dear, that road doesn't go any farther up that way. It only goes to a big house up on that estate up there, it only goes that length and there's no another farm on the road up that way. And it's no worth your while going up that way. But anyway, it'll no matter. You need something for your bairns, do you? Well, there's plenty here. Everything you want.'

So she went; brother dear, she gave the woman everything she wanted, tea and sugar, meat, flesh, cheese, milk, everything she required!

She said, 'Does your man smoke?'

'Oh, God bless you, cratur! My man never had a smoke for three days.'

'Wait a minute, my man smokes.' And it was thon bogie twist*. She wrapped it in a twist on her arm, cut it off with a knife, and said, 'That'll keep him going for the night.'

The Traveller woman went down on her knees and blessed her. The farm woman had given her as much as would have done her for a week.

'Now,' she said, 'this is our ground till you come to the crossroads, it's all owned by my man. And, you'll need a place for your tent tonight, won't you? Go up the road on your left-hand side and you'll see the ruins of an old thatched house. Now, you go in that ruins and put your tent

* thon bogie twist – pipe tobacco in a roll not available today

up there and make your bairns some supper. And there's a stack of straw across the road – help yourself to as much as you want for your beds! And burn any sticks you see in about the old house.'

The Traveller woman was in tears, brother dear, with gladness! And she felt kind of darlin' with this glass of brandy, see!

She said, 'Are you hungry yourself?'

'Never mind me, missus, I'm mair interested in my weans getting a wee bite.'

'Well, look, you go down,' she said, 'and tell your man to put his camp up – I know what a camp is, I know what you do – put your camp in the ruins of the old house. There's plenty of ground and at the back of the dyke there's a wee well, you'll get plenty of water.' And she gave her as much as she could carry, she said, 'Wait a minute, will you manage to carry some potatoes?' Into the shed – she came out with about two stone of Golden Wonders. 'That'll make a supper to the bairns.'

The woman was loaded, brother dear, by the time she got to the road end. The man, he's sitting with the three wee weans at the road end with the barra.

'God bless my soul and body,' he said, 'that woman's no a while!'

But at last she came down. She had everything from the woman that she could carry.

He said, 'Did you get anything at all?'

'Wheesht,' she said, 'that's an angel up there, tha-that-that's God up there in that farm, that's an angel from heaven! I got mair from that woman up there than I got for the last three weeks. And she said we've to go up the road to the ruins of the old house and put our tent up, and there's plenty straw and . . .' she explained to the man.

The man was quite happy. 'You never got . . .'

'Smoke!' She pulled a thing like a bit of rope out of her pocket. She says, 'Look!'

'Oh God bless you!' he said, 'I'm going to make another two baskets for her tomorrow before I go away! You'll go up and give them to her for nothing.'

She said, 'The woman's no wanting any mair baskets. The woman's quite happy.'

So the man got all this stuff and he packed it in the barra. And up he goes, see! He pulls into this wee old broken down house. Oh, in minutes he kindles the fire with rotten boards. And on his snotem he boils the can, the woman boils flesh and makes scones, gives these with cheese to the weans. In two minutes the wee weans were full and they're playing on the dyke. The man pulls in his wee barra – off with his campsticks, up with his wee bow tent, brother dear, crosses the road for two bunches of corn straw! He put them into the tent, and with the bits of blankets the woman made the bed. The wee weans were playing themselves, had had plenty to eat.

Now, the farm woman had given her about seven pounds of smoked pork off the cleek. She said, 'Johnnie, brother dear, God that I had something to boil those tatties in for them weans. If I had an old cannister – anything lying about would do – I could put a wire in it . . .' She had no pot or anything.

'Ach well, we can't help it,' he said, 'we'll just have to do without them. We'll maybe get a pot in the morning some place on the road.'

He went away round the back of this wee house, pulling bits of boards out, raking around the old house. He found bits of old furniture and bits of old beds and things lying in the old house. Somebody had walked out and the house had become neglected. He went round the back of this wee shed round the back of the house. He was pulling bits of rotten boards and he looked – in below the shed sitting in the corner was a three-footed pot! A metal three-footed pot with a handle on it, three rings round on it and every foot about four inches long. Rusty.

He put his hand away in and he pulled it out, he looked at the pot, tested it – 'Oh, dear-dear,' he said, 'there's a bad pot!'* Will she be pleased with that! Wait a minute!' Back he goes to her, 'Would that boil your tatties?'

'Oh, Johnnie, brother dear,' she said, 'a three-footed pot – all my life I've wanted a pot like that.' It was all the go in those days. 'Brother, you clean that to me and I'll never part with it.'

'I'll clean it up to you in a minute,' he said.

The man filled his pipe and he put on a fire, hung the pot on the snotem till it was blood-red. And he went to the burn with it, got a sod and scoured it till it shone, shone like a new shilling. And he came back.

He said, 'Will that do you now?'

'Oh,' she said. 'That's a bad pot!'

She filled it with Golden Wonders and put the meat into it. She brought it to a boil, it boiled in no time at all! She sat down, fed the wee weans as much as they could eat, and whatever was left over in the pot she emptied it into a cloot, put it in her basket. She went to the burn and cleaned the pot out. And she put it opposite the head of her bed on two stones outside the tent.

She said, 'Ah, brother dear, all the days of my life I've wanted a pot to make soup for my weans. I'll never part with that.'

* a bad pot! – a splendid one

So it got kind of late at night and they went to bed.

The man pulled down the door of their bow tent, left a wee bit open. He's lying at the door, she's lying at the back and the three weans are at the back, lying sound, their legs stretched out – after a good tightener*! And he's lying smoking his pipe, and his bonnet's lying at the front; see, he kept his pipe and bonnet at the door.

But he must have dovered off to sleep, when all in a minute she gave him a bump with her elbow, 'Johnnie!'

'What?'

'My pot – there's somebody bingin my pot avrie†.'

'Wha-what's wrong, woman?'

'There's somebody bingin my pot avrie, I heard the handle – somebody's lifting it.'

'Tsst, awa, there's naebody near your pot, woman. Go back to sleep!'

'Honest to God,' she said, 'I heard my pot – somebody's lifting it off the stanes.'

'You and that mental pot,' he said, 'God that I had never seen that pot if that's the way you're going to carry on!'

But he lay down to sleep, and she fell asleep.

But the pot, brother! – 'clink', off the stones and away! 'Deedle-daddle, deedle-daddle,' out to the road and off, up the road and away the pot went! The pot's toddling on, boy, at a good heavy lick! Up the pot goes to the bene kane‡, up the drive, in the door, round the back into the kitchen, right on the floor.

Now what was on at the castle but a big shoot§ the next morning! And the cook was working late to get all the

---

* good tightener – feed to fill your belly
† bingin . . . avrie – stealing
‡ bene kane – laird's house, castle
§ big shoot – grand hunt

dinners made for the guests the next day. Now he wants to boil something and he can't get anything.

He said, 'I told the master I was needing pots and things; I've run out of pots.' And he looks – sitting on the floor, brother, the metal pot! 'He must have bought one and left it there for me.'

The cook lifted it, packed all his beef into it, as much as he could pack into this pot – beautiful beef for the guests the next day – put it on to boil. He brought it to a boil, sat and read a book till it was ready, put the pot down on the floor to cool. He went away to his bed after everything was set.

And when he went away to his bed, brother – 'click', up with the handle of the pot, out the pot goes, out through the door. 'Deedle-daddle,' out the drive, down the road back the way it came, right back down, crosses the road, in to the back of the tent, up on top of the stones, down 'squeak'. Sat there.

Night passed by, the man got up in the morning, kindled the fire, hung the can on for the tea. The woman got up, washed her face and hands.

She said, 'I'll go round to the pot, I hope nobody's been at my pot – maybe it was rats during the night.' She looked – 'In the name of God, Johnnie, come here till you see this. Come here! You didn't believe me about the pot, now!'

'God curse you and the pot!' he said.

'Come here,' she said, 'do you believe me now about the pot!' There it was, brother – packed to the mouth with flesh! Beautiful boiled beef. The old man was mesmerized. They didn't know what to do about it.

He said, 'Woman, I'll tell you something – that pot's haunted – that never came . . .'

'Tsst,' she said, 'probably somebody came in at night-time and they felt pity for us. They put it in the pot for us,' she made up an excuse. Gravy was floating on the top, solid on top. 'Well,' she said. 'I'll tell you something, I've got two or three things to wash for the weans today and I don't feel like moving on.'

He said, 'What are we moving on for? The woman said we could bide here for a couple of days. I've plenty of tobacco and there's plenty of sticks here, you've plenty of meat to do the weans. We'll bide for another day or two anyway. I'll maybe wander up the road and see if I can get two-three wands*.' The wee weans were playing away to their heart's content.

But anyway, the woman put on the pot again – oh, they had plenty of meat! She boiled another pot of tatties to all this beef. Not a body ever came about them.

But the day passed by, night came again, bedtime. The woman scoured her pot. If she scoured it clean the first night, she scoured it better the next night. She built a special bit at her head, right at her head close to the tent cloth. She put the pot outside, because Travellers always kept their dishes outside. She put the pot out on the two stones. The man went into bed, he lay down, his pipe and his bonnet were at his head. He lay smoking for a while. He must have dovered to sleep again. He was lying for about an hour and the moon came out.

'Johnnie!'

'What, woman – what!'

She says, 'My pot!'

'Take the pot to bed with you,' he said, 'if you think – there's naebody near your pot!'

'I heard it,' she said, 'it's rattling again. Go up and see!'

He got up, pulled his trousers up and he went round – the pot's sitting on the stone. 'Your pot's sitting on the stone,

nobody touched your pot.'

* two-three wands – some willows to make a basket

Back to bed, he lay down again. But an hour, about an hour passed by.

'Clink', handle gets up, off goes the pot, off the stones and away again! Out down the wee pad, out to the main road, 'deedle-daddle' off to the castle again. But this time it didn't go into the kitchen. It went round to the front door and up the stair – right up to the bene cowl's* bedroom. And this bene cowl was a miser, a real miser, you see! He didn't trust banks or anything, he kept all his money in the house. He hid it in jars here and jars there and wee puckles here, wee puckles there.

So this night he took a thought that folk were going to steal it from him. He said, 'I'll have to find a suitable hiding place so they'll no' get it. If I had some – a box to put it in so's to keep it all together! Some of it might go a-missing and I'll never know. I think they're all asleep, I think I'll collect it all.' So he collected it all from his hiding places and he put it on the floor. 'Now,' he said, 'if I could see something to put it in,' and he looked, brother – sitting on the floor beside him was the pot! He said, 'The very thing. The *very* thing! The cook must have forgotten and left it sitting there, he'll never know where it went.' He packed all the gold into the pot, half sovereigns and gold sovereigns, packed it all into the pot, carried and put it below the corner of his bed, put a cloot on the top of it. On with his nightwear, his nightcap and into bed. Now he's sound asleep, sound to the world.

But when he was asleep for two hours, 'click', up goes the handle of the pot. 'Deedle-daddle', out go the three legs, canny out the door, down the stairs, out the drive and away! Down the road, back all the way it came, back to the wee house, in to the back of the tent, up on the two stones, down goes the handle – quiet, not a word, pot's sitting.

* bene cowl's – laird's, rich man's

The man and woman woke up in the morning. On with his can, he made a drop of tea. She got up, usual thing – washed her face and made tea.

She goes round the side of the tent, 'Johnnie, did you put a cloot on top of my pot? Dirty cloot on top of my pot – you know I make meat in it to my weans!'

'Woman,' he said, 'I wasn't near your pot.'

She said, 'Some of you weans must have put a cloot on top of it – you can't put cloots on my pot, for making meat to my weans!' She pulled the cloot back and looked. The woman nearly fainted – it was packed to the mouth with gold sovereigns and half sovereigns. 'Johnnie, come here, come till you see this, could you come till you see this! I told you now about my pot . . .'

The man looked. 'God bless my soul and body,' he said, 'where did that come from? I'll tell you something: that's an enchanted pot, woman. I'll tell you the best thing – you'd better get rid of it!'

'Aye! I'm getting rid of my pot. You're no wise, man!'

The man went in and pulled a shawl off the bed (I suppose it was only two shawls they had on the bed), and he spread it out. He couped the gold sovereigns in the shawl, tied it in a knot and packed it into his wee barra.

He said, 'It'll be too dubious if we go away the day. We'll wait till the morn. If nobody turns up we'll know that everything's all right.' The man put a handful of straw in the bottom of the barra, put the shawl full of gold sovereigns in the barra and covered it with straw. 'Now,' he said, 'in the morn if it's still there when we get up, we'll say we don't know anything about it.' The woman took her pot and put it up in the back on the stones.

So everything passed well till the night. They went to bed again. The man lay down smoking. He was lying for a good while.

Then, 'Johnnie,' she said, 'Johnnie?'

'What is it noo, woman?'

'My pot.'

'God curse you and your pot,' he said. 'I told you to take the pot and put it round your neck or put it at your head and keep the pot! Do you no' think the pot's done enough for you? What mair do ye want it tae do . . . *I hope in God, in the morn when you get up, you'll never see it again!*'

But anyway, the woman fell back asleep. Morning came and they got up. The man got up, kindled the fire and made a wee sip of tea. She got up and the first thing she did when she got up, she went round the side of the tent – na, it was gone. No pot.

She said, 'Maybe some . . .'

'Maybe some of the weans,' he said, 'did you ask the wee weans – did you take your mummy's pot away?'

'No-o, no, Daddy, we never saw the pot, no, we never saw it.'

'Well,' she said, 'I put it there last night.'

They searched the house, ate the ruins.*

She said, 'I would rather have the pot as all the money . . . I'll bet you a pound there's no money!'

He said, 'What are you talking about – money – that was only something that happened, we just imagined it. It'll never happen again.'

The man went to the barra and he pulled back the straw – there was the shawl packed to the mouth, the gold sovereigns were still there. But they searched and they searched and they searched, the pot was gone. And the pot was never seen again.

The next day the man packed his wee bit tent on the back of his barra and bade farewell to the glen, he never went

---

* ate the ruins – couldn't have been more thorough in their search.

back again. They went down to the town, he bought a big property to himself, and from that day to this day, they never wanted for another thing. But never again did they get word of the pot!

And that's the last of my story.

When the man said, 'I hope in God, in the morn when you get up, you'll never see it again!' that was the spell broken. His words were potent because he was the one who had got the pot, you see! My Uncle Duncan told me that, my mother's brother. Aye, he was good at the stories all right.

Glossary

Traveller Cant and Scots words

awa	away; don't be stupid
awfae	awful
bairns	children
bachal	wild young man
bairn	child
barra	pram converted into a handcart
barrikit	large dome-shaped tent with compartments, barricade
ben	into
bene	good, fine
burk	kidnap
camp	tent
canny	gently; carefully
carlin	long-stemmed, durable (heather)
ceilidh	song and story get-together
clartiest	most untidy, dirtiest
cleek	large kitchen hook suspended from rafters for hanging meat or fish to smoke
cloot	cloth
couped	emptied, tipped
couples	rafters
crack	chat, tell short stories
cratur	creature, dear one
creel	handmade basket
cruisie	open lamp with a rush wick
cry	call
dae	do
dinnae	don't
doubt	fear, expect
dovered	dozed
dram	measure, drink of whisky
droll	queer

fabbat	tired
fairing	complete
fank	a sheepfold
feared	afraid
flesh	freshly butchered meat
gadgie	man
gien	gave
Golden Wonders	the best Scottish potatoes
greet	cry, weep
groany	decrepit
haet	nothing
hantle	people, folk
hoolits	owls
hurl	pull, ride around
jeejament	curse
keek	peep
kent	knew
knowe	hillock
mair	more
messages	groceries
mutch	jute sack apron, old-fashioned frilly bonnet
no	not
noo	now
o	of
oxter	the upper underarm
pad	narrow leg of the path
piece	a slice of bread
puckle	small amount
shanned	ashamed, embarrassed
shelfie	chaffinch
skelp	strike, hit
snotem	iron crook for hanging pots over the open fire
stanes	stones
stotting	walking sprightly
tatties	potatoes
thon	that, a type you wouldn't see today
timey	while spent (with someone)
two-three	a few
wands	wild willow strands suitable for basket weaving
wap	wrap
waste	remote
wean	child, wee one
wheesht	quiet, listen!
yir	your
ye're	you're
yirsel	yourself